UNTYING THE
APRON

DAUGHTERS REMEMBER
MOTHERS OF THE 1950s

ESSENTIAL ANTHOLOGIES SERIES 4

Canada Council for the Arts **Conseil des Arts du Canada**

ONTARIO ARTS COUNCIL
CONSEIL DES ARTS DE L'ONTARIO

50 YEARS OF ONTARIO GOVERNMENT SUPPORT OF THE ARTS
50 ANS DE SOUTIEN DU GOUVERNEMENT DE L'ONTARIO AUX ARTS

Guernica Editions Inc. acknowledges the support of the
Canada Council for the Arts and the Ontario Arts Council.
The Ontario Arts Council is an agency of the Government of Ontario.

We acknowledge the financial support of the Government of Canada
through the Canada Book Fund (CBF) for our publishing activities.

UNTYING THE
APRON

DAUGHTERS REMEMBER
MOTHERS OF THE 1950s

EDITED BY
LORRI NEILSEN GLENN

GUERNICA
TORONTO—BUFFALO—BERKELEY—LANCASTER (U.K.)
2013

Lorri Neilsen Glenn, editor
Michael Mirolla, general editor
Interior design by Jill Ronsley
Guernica Editions Inc.
P.O. Box 76080, Abbey Market, Oakville, (ON), Canada L6M 3H5
2250 Military Road, Tonawanda, N.Y. 14150-6000 U.S.A.

Distributors:
University of Toronto Press Distribution,
5201 Dufferin Street, Toronto (ON), Canada M3H 5T8
Gazelle Book Services, White Cross Mills, High Town,
Lancaster LA1 4XS U.K.

Second edition.
Printed in Canada.

Legal Deposit—First Quarter
Library of Congress Catalog Card Number: 2012951762

Library and Archives Canada Cataloguing in Publication
Untying the apron : daughters remember mothers of the
1950s / Lorri Neilsen Glenn, editor.

(Essential anthologies series ; 4)
Also issued in electronic format.
ISBN 978-1-55071-729-7

1. Mothers—Literary collections. 2. Canadian literature (English)—
21st century. I. Neilsen, Lorri II. Series: Essential anthologies series
(Toronto, Ont.) ; 4

PS8237.M64U57 2013   C810.8'035252   C2012-907091-2

Contents

GETTING READY 187

ACKNOWLEDGEMENTS 227

CONTRIBUTORS 231

PREFACE

IN THESE PAGES, poets, novelists, journalists, playwrights, and writers of creative nonfiction and memoir gather our recollections of the women we knew as mothers. How do we, as adults, remember them now? As we look back, what can we learn from this largely uncelebrated generation about how to survive and thrive, to adapt and resist, how to live in a world we're given?

This collection of prose and poetry was several years in the making. It is filled with singular details of the lives of complex women whose lives, at the time, seemed ordinary. None were ordinary. All had a story, and all were at once living out cultural mores of the time and making their own mark: there are no June Cleavers or Margaret Andersons here. I think of a schoolmate's mother who was always pleasant, polite, and contained. After she died, my friend found her mother's trunk of handwritten journals filled with vituperation and fury, four decades of venting about neighbours, friends, and family. So many mothers, including my own, were whip-smart and creative, practical and savvy, and they chose—or they had no choice—to live under the thumb of a husband's or family's demands. They might work outside the home for "pin money" in order to pay for braces or clarinet or violin lessons; such earnings enabled the real breadwinner's pride to remain intact. Single mothers—and there were many in the 1950s—were often invisible in the rural communities of my youth. Yet they, too, watched while we, the daughters, often blithe and self-absorbed, went off into the open horizon of the 1960s and 70s, rarely looking back.

I began soliciting and gathering pieces for the collection when my own mother's death was imminent and I was preparing for my own grief. The mother/daughter bond is often intense and fraught, yet it is a fierce bond.

My sister and I each had our own complicated relationship with our mother, and we mourn her still. (A note: two sets of sisters write about their mothers here).

Consider this collection a kaffeeklatsch, post-war mothers gathered to reveal their resilience, hope, anger, frustration, madness, despair, happiness, humour, zaniness, mystery, and light. Here the reader will find new Canadians, war brides, farm women, white-gloved socialites, compliant suburban princesses, and rebellious tough broads. Here are women who could pry their arm from a wringer washer in time to make a grilled cheese sandwich, repair a crinoline or knit a curling sweater, who boiled vegetables until they were grey, fixed the tractor, played concert piano, served delicacies such as pigs in a blanket on the Silver Birch on Sunday, and twisted their daughters' hair into pincurls as the family watched *Ed Sullivan*.

As editor, I have many people to thank. First, I am grateful for the fine writing and patience of the 55 contributors who waited as I combed through submissions, edited material, and searched for a publisher. Your candor, grace and generosity—all hallmarks, as well, of your fine writing—made this collection possible. Writer and anthologist Marjorie Anderson provided early advice and support at a critical time, and I thank her. I am grateful to Ruth Ann Brown, whose skills, patience, and attention to detail were crucial as I wrestled with word processing demands. Lindsay Brown suggested I approach Michael Mirolla, whose enthusiasm for the book enabled me to let contributors know that Guernica Editions would be its home; my thanks to them both. I want to acknowledge, too, my decades-long friend, Pat Clifford, whose humour and mother stories buoyed me, and who insisted on completing revisions to her contribution before her death in 2008.

I want to thank my sister, Allison Marion, as well as my husband Allan, both of whom understand deeply the importance of this project. I dedicate this collection to my mother, Grace, to my Aunt Kay, and to all mothers.

—Lorri Neilsen Glenn

KEEPING UP

DEBORAH KERR, co-starring in MGM's "Quo Vadis"—in color by Technicolor

DEBORAH KERR . . . Lustre-Creme presents one of the 12 women voted as having the world's loveliest hair. Deborah Kerr uses Lustre-Creme Shampoo to care for her glamorous hair.

The Most Beautiful Hair in the World is kept at its loveliest with
Lustre-Creme Shampoo

Yes, Deborah Kerr uses Lustre-Creme Shampoo— high praise for this unique shampoo, because beautiful hair is vital to the glamour-careers of Hollywood stars.

Deborah Kerr is one of 12 women named by "Modern Screen" and famed Hollywood hair stylists as having the most beautiful hair in the world.

You, too, will notice a glorious difference in your hair after a Lustre-Creme Shampoo. Under the spell of its rich, lanolin-blessed lather, your hair shines, behaves, is eager to curl. Hair dulled by soap abuse, dusty with dandruff, now is fragrantly clean. Hair robbed of its sheen now glows with new highlights. Lustre-Creme lathers lavishly in hardest water, needs no special after-rinse.

The beauty-blend cream shampoo with lanolin. Jars or tubes.

FAMOUS HOLLYWOOD STARS USE LUSTRE-CREME SHAMPOO FOR GLAMOROUS HAIR

Keeping Up

Daphne Marlatt

keeping up appearances
keeping up with the Joneses
keep those home fires burning
keep yourself up to the mark

each daughter's avenue back to her mother in the 50s must surely be singular, despite the commonality of a particular decade. so many factors criss-cross family history: region, class, ethnic background, individual tolerance for the stresses of the period.

but why avenue? it was a period of expanding roads, subdivisions, highways, bridges, a focus on growth, transportation and long distance communication despite the Cold War threat. a focus not just on survival but on "getting somewhere," making your mark in the expanding economy that followed the destruction and losses of the War. a period of striving for some benchmark called success and recognized as such by your community.

the past is never easy to gain entry on without the present interfering—indeed, from this vantage point half a century later, how could our view of the 50s not be coloured by all that has happened since? certain aspects seem more prominent, perhaps because we sense their continuing impact on us. pausing at one of those momentary intersections where past and present collide, i am triggered by a phrase that opens up a network of associations. keeping up and losers keepers, keeping the beat and refusing to be your sister's keeper. negotiating the contained rock of a mother's depression and the ecstatic beat of rock 'n' roll. the 50s: between a hard rock and a cool place.

like mother like daughter
and how it became unlike
heading into the 60s.

in the 50s Mom was contained by Hallmark platitudes, by the sanctions of the Church where good wives and mothers "knew their place," a lot lower than the angels, unless you were young, beautiful, and (sexually) innocent. still, you covered your "crowning glory" with a hat and a little veil, you wore gloves to cover your work-sullied hands, you wore smart new clothes at Easter to show your respect for the ever-present eyes of God (and all the eyes that were stand-ins for Him). you and the other women arranged flowers on the altar, organized garden parties to raise funds for the Church, Christmas parties for the children, Church suppers after meetings where the men spoke and the women washed stacks of dishes with their glove-uncovered hands.

you were a good wife and mother if you were constrained by what the neighbours might say, or the mothers at the PTA, neighbours at bridge clubs, volunteers at sundry charities—a good woman performs good deeds. and for entertainment you went to the cinema with your husband or your eldest daughter and watched MGM musicals set in romantic Paris about respectable (or not-so-respectable) young girls of humble circumstance who find their wealthy true loves. in "real life," at coffee klatches and Church suppers, during small talk, hands held to mouth, raised eyebrows at a name, it was gossiped about, or there were intimations that, not all the women on your block were sufficiently respectable.

innuendo, oblique suggestion
policing "suggestiveness"
and "straying eyes"
discretion was a word to live up to
but so was attractive when you
looked in the mirror to see
how you measured up

Ask Yourself: Do I Please my Husband?

mirrors not just on walls or dressing tables or the outside reflected in plate glass windows adorning the newest split-level homes. mirrors on the pages of *Good Housekeeping, Family Circle, Ladies' Home Journal* where advice was freely dispensed at every turn. *The right way to cream your face ... How to keep your husband happy.*

community was still intact and social mirroring enforced the unspoken norms. making "a spectacle of yourself" not just a no-no, but a consensual taboo. on the other side of that chasm lay the realm of the social pariah, a place of utter solitude. pax Nathaniel Hawthorne. pax Thomas Hardy.

Have you tried to correct your faults?

the good mother raised her daughter to be like herself—cued to what was "expected," cute perhaps, but not too cute. sociable and effervescent like Doris Day. but sexually contained and visibly correct.

Your children's behaviour will reflect on you, their mother.

gave her daughters Sears catalogues to dream over and cut-out dolls to dress in their paper wardrobes with little tabs folding over shoulders and arms, around waist and thighs. flouncy dresses, tailored suits. suitable attire, in short, for the various occasions they were destined for. oh there she goes in her jodhpurs and riding boots for horse-riding forays (no one we knew in North Van rode horses). there she goes to her fiancé's office party in her little black cocktail dress with the sweetheart neckline and string of pearls (cocktail parties a necessary part of the class code). there she goes in her Ethel Merman bathing costume to the beach. in her floor-length gown and mink stole to the theatre, or failing mink, muskrat (who went to any of the "little theatre" shows in floor-length gowns? to opera downtown perhaps, but that was considered snobbish and highbrow on our block). all of it offered as dress-up rehearsal for the expectations of "grown-up life." (oh the mothers had expectations of their daughters that preceded the advent of Chuck Berry, Little

Richard, and Presley in their daughters' radio-tuned, hit chart and TV-broadcast lives, the new "youth culture" they were dancing to streamed its alternative images across the border.)

Ask Yourself: Am I a Responsive, Well-adjusted Wife?

the upwardly mobile middle-class mother, exhorted by ads and articles in the daily papers, on buses, in magazines, to keep up with the latest convenience, improve her image, her home, her family's standing. these exhortations making her, "*The Little Woman*," making her over in the image of *an expert buyer*: not just a practiced eye and a good memory for prices, but full-blown fantasy scaling the class walls as if her very identity depended on it.

snapping up bargains
stretching the budget

and the supermarkets went up—all those aisles and choices, wheeled carts to fill and a car to carry it all home in. the new abundance of brand names competing with wartime memories of scarcity. stocking the kitchen cupboards in case of disaster: a missile attack, a hydrogen bomb, a polio epidemic. "you never know ..."

and still, after all that, failing to "keep up"

underneath the boom and glitter, under the newly paved roads and subdivisions, the unspoken simmered. buried conflicts, unacknowledged fears and failures, secret drinking, hidden losses, covered over with a carefully-lipsticked smile. a new perm. a new hat. "putting a good face on things."

It is up to the wife to take the first step by enhancing her desirability as a companion. because if she didn't, another, the "other," woman might step in. no quarters given in the competition for available men, with newly attractive divorcees, young war widows still around. "a good man" was hard to find and, once found, it was up to her to keep him. in the new subdivisions there was talk of bedroom parties, wife-swapping. at cocktail parties, the secret messages of eyes. to keep the home fires burning, you had to be on your guard against other women.

... the wise wife and mother always remembers that her husband comes first.

after trying to measure up and somehow failing, after making fun of those "old biddies" who policed their circle, after crying "hypocrite" at the gap between what was espoused and what enacted, after bemoaning his long hours at the office and the long commute, after finding her daughters badly-behaved and ungrateful, she lapsed into alternating rage and silence. house-bound in a worn housedress—a chronically exhausted housewife. a domestic casualty confined to home.

and this despite the new communications networks everywhere— all so much hype, so much hot air. and inside, at cocktail parties, in grocery lineups, at Church socials, so much small talk. because what was left unspoken, the common (if she'd only known) inadequacies and wounds, the usual abandonments and unmothering, were never broached, never spoken. that impermeable wall still erect in the 50s between what was public and what was private, even within the four walls of the family home. it would take two decades for consciousness-raising groups to come together so that daughters could share their own inadequacies and wounds and later, perhaps, begin to talk openly with their mothers. but, unless she could trust a friend who didn't put her husband first, who would break through the "good woman" wall between them, each mother in the 50s was on her own.

Last Summer in the Old Craig House

E. Alex Pierce

Musk melon, moth skirt, with those skin-like petals
that come in pink and white. Mauve pink, for musk,
our mother, that summer our brother was born.

Gold spun hair on the gun-metal green lilacs, put there
to help the fairies build their houses. And fairy-rings
she found in the mossy woods. She was certain of it.

We were two lost princesses
travelling with her in her last bid for freedom

while she still ran wild
in the meadows and woods-roads

traipsing us down through the salt marsh
to sit on Craig's Beach and have royal cups of tea,
red Kool-aid that ran in streams

down our white shirts. It was our last summer
in that house, the end of our reign—
he came in August, late August.

They put a Union Jack out on the clothesline
up the road.

To give birth—to a son.

Lying in that brass iron bed—
now, she was Queen.

SLINGBACKS

Myrna Garanis

I scold my mother
for wearing slingbacks,
as we head for an outdoor stage
with plenty of steps to climb.

She's 86 and spry, cataracts
cloud her eyes yet she won't stoop to flats.
Wears her favorite beige and browns,
spindly size sevens, stylish, compared
to my Clarks.

Standing five feet tall,
she declares she needs their height.
Besides, this is a dress-up affair.
She glances disapproving
at my uncoiffed hair.

Turned out
in matching skirt and blouse,
fresh perm, pearl brooch,
and screw-back earrings,
she lets my appearance ride.
I'm the only available chauffeur.

We wobble up the stairs. She
accepts each stranger's outstretched
arm. Safely seated, she inspects
all dresses in our row, recommends
one or two broad-brimmed hats,
straightens her purse and back,
then leans over to me and whispers
that I might do the same.

COMBUSTION

Lorri Neilsen Glenn

And so the nuns put my little brother Jack into the furnace, and that was that. My mother doesn't know until she wakes, the white shoes a whisper by her bed, my father's voice cold sand in her ear. And I, at home, curled near the heat register, Gram despairing that I won't eat. Won't eat. Waiting for the baby. Snowball sits on the back of the chesterfield, watching what wind does in the claws of bare trees, drifts outside too high and wilding for her paws, too high for me and my snowsuit. Too high, too cold. And the black phone on the wall. And no baby. Fine then, no soup. *They decided*, she says now, fifty years away, as we sit on the deck, our skin inhaling summer-waning sun. *The holy Trinity. Doctor, nun, husband. Dead of winter. They could have waited until I saw my son's face.* She stuffs out her cigarette, rolls her head back. That distance—where she goes. I reach, grasp only the howl of storms in the small railway town, fist of cold at the door in winter, maw of Main Street under high clouds and summer dust. My father's voice at supper—*they fired the stationmaster today:* image of a man tied to a pole over a bonfire. The July parade: crepe paper, my white peaked hat and apron, the Old Dutch Cleanser woman. Joey, hobbling beside me, brown-fringed hat and holster. The water tower the highest thing in the world at the end of the road. Drums. And the Switzer girls on their tricycles ahead of us, gone the next winter. Fire, their whole house down. Clang of the coal stove, my father shovelling at dawn. Heat. Cold. Mother. Gram. Cat. And the empty space where a baby was going to be. I could pull out the old Brownie photos, crisp and snapping from their little crow-wing tabs, burn those into my mind. But how to go back on my own. To go where she goes, even to the edge. She pulls out her lighter again. The DuMaurier, a small white finger in her mouth, sparks. Ash. *Lying there, cut from my gut to my ribs. Sick from ether. Out cold. And he comes home from Hinton in time to tell them to go ahead. Dispose of the body. Small town. Small hospital. And you at home, waiting.* Stillborn. A brother. Out the chimney into the air, the whole town breathing him. Her smoke drifts off the deck toward the trees, white mark in the air, a wavering trail.

Silver Bangles

Margaret Zielinski

Always a cluster of them round her wrist—
mother tinkled when she moved, when she ran
upstairs or cuddled me and tucked me into bed. As I played
I listened for that sound, knew I was safe.

They jingled on Mondays as she washed mountains
of sheets and pegged them out to blow
on lines crisscrossing the garden
as she shovelled coal from the shed
and heaved buckets into the house,
as she stoked the fires father wanted in every room,
tried to dust away the soot clouding air,
laid the table at noon, again at twenty to six,
as she hurried to have hot milk and two digestive biscuits
waiting for father as he returned from the pub at ten past ten.

After he died, Mother took the bus
to Townsend's, the jeweller on Victoria Road
and told him to cut off those bangles.
They tinkled as he pried them from her swollen hands.

My Mother Does Not Appear

Sheila Norgate

In most of my childhood photos, my mother is on the other side of the glass, staring down into her black plastic Brownie camera, directing us with her one free arm, trying to apply some measure of influence over the surging tide of her life.

In 1942, at the height of Britain's involvement in World War Two and just shy of her 20th birthday, she entered nursing school in Manchester, England. The training was exacting, cruel, and stiff with discipline. A few months into the blood and bandages she met my father, a Canadian infantryman on leave. Together they came down with that strain of urgent attraction peculiar to times of battle. Their courtship was truncated, snatched from the war effort one day at a time, and they were married on March 11, 1943 at the seaside town of Blackpool.

Now the official property of the Dominion of Canada, she was conscripted into the Women's Division of the Royal Canadian Air Force whose motto it was *"to serve that men may fly."* Her slender, burgundy, clothbound Service Book reports the date of enlistment as 13.7.43 and her surname as that of her newly-minted husband *Norgate*. Soon all of her original names would evaporate; brokered in exchange for standing as a married woman.

Like her nursing career, her service in the RCAF was brief. The only other notation in the booklet appears under Miscellaneous Entries: *"Remittance to Canada 15.3.44."* Three months into her first pregnancy, she was packaged up and dispatched overseas with a shifting cargo of other queasy English war brides. Two uniforms in two years, neither one broken in.

My mother's dreams for a fresh start in her new country washed up hard on the craggy shores of Nova Scotia's Pier 21. Canadian women were not pleased to see this consignment of girlish British thieves no matter how many official pamphlets of welcome were produced by the government of the day. In addition to diminished supplies of sugar, steel, and silk stockings, there was a dire shortage of young men, and these foreign girls had claimed for themselves some of Canada's finest. It didn't help that she lamented, often and audibly, the substandard quality of North American wares.

She kept to herself; a lonely young mother in a foreign land with a mounting inventory of babies and a husband she hadn't recognized since he returned from active duty. Within the fertile, cramped quarters of the first six years of her marriage, she had three children, two shy of her eventual complement of five. Prodded by the homemaking guides of her day, and fuelled by an urgency to outstrip the pace of her sorrow, she fashioned smocked dresses and wool suits with matching caps, hand-knit sweaters, blankets, booties; all part of a watertight cover-up. The side of us that faced the world was bright and polished and well turned out, but at home we lived on the dark, inhospitable half of our family's moon, on a terrain pockmarked by the deep yawning footprint of the Second World War.

Her one solace was late-night sewing. She would bow to her creamy beige Singer machine, gathering a scrap of time at the end of her day, an oasis of fabric and thread. From the top bunk in the upstairs front bedroom I could hear the gentle hypnotic hum, the starting and stopping, the metal pressed to cloth, as she engineered French seamed highways; twin rails of promise to ride out on beyond the clawed grasping reach of her life. The small silver foot lifted up and down, capturing a steady stream of textile; a march on the spot, her tissue paper patterns fragile maps leading nowhere.

The stream of homemade garb intended for her children slowed to a trickle by the time I was ten and dried up altogether when the last hand-me down was handed down to me. That's when she began to sew for herself; one dress after another after another as though, if they were tied together like prison bed sheets, she might be able to lower herself out the window, down to the ground.

She taught herself how to make hats to go with these dresses, travelling on Saturday mornings to the millinery supply store on Bay Street in downtown Toronto where she joined a band of other women straining their dreams through muslin forms. There were never enough occasions to warrant wearing these elegant and beautifully made dresses and most of them hung unworn, in her closet, waiting, like her, in the dark, with their matching hats stored directly above them in pristine elliptical boxes.

Mom stopped making hats and dresses altogether in 1973 when she moved from Toronto to Drayton, a small dozing farm community in Southwestern Ontario. Her Drayton social calendar was impossibly lean, even thinner than Toronto's, and the unworn dresses piled up in her closet like resentful firstborn children protesting late arrivals. She lost her appetite for fine feminine sewing and turned her attention instead to garments more suitable for escape: simple elastic-waist trousers and loosely-tailored shirts.

Lead by Mom's ceaseless yearning for a return to saltwater, my parents moved to the Canadian west coast in 1981 and then separated shortly afterwards. My father returned my mother to the seaside and then he wandered away.

She spent her last years living alone in a trailer park in Langford, British Columbia. Practicing a frugality familiar only to those who have lived through war, she had managed to save enough money from her inadequate separation allowance to purchase the smallest trailer in the park. It had been used as an office on a construction site but now it offered my mother the only rooms of her own she had ever known.

She stopped curling or colouring her hair and cut it herself using the same pair of scissors she had used to cut ours. Her style was short and neat with bangs as straight as a ruler running across her forehead. She joined a gardening group in Victoria and on her allotted patch of ground raised flawless, organic vegetables. At harvest time every year she became unreachable for weeks at a stretch, busy turning her earth bound charges into the soups and stews and sauces that would carry her through the rest of the year. She vacuum-sealed everything in plastic denominations of one and placed them in her freezer, carefully documenting every entry in a log.

At the time of her death in 1995, her freezer was impossibly full. The demand had not kept pace with the supply, and even though she carefully re-arranged the inventory every year by putting the newest submissions under the older ones, there was far too much food for one small-boned English girl, eating alone, to manage.

Like her freezer, her tall maple sewing cabinet was packed to overflowing with possibilities: patterns by McCalls and Butterick (but *never* Simplicity!) and remnants of cloth folded with military precision, some dating back to the days of Lester Pearson.

When the ambulance attendants arrived to take her unconscious body to the hospital, the dollhouse scale of her trailer proved troublesome. The stretcher would not fit into the tiny bedroom and the men had to hoist her up under her arms and knees, one on either side to carry her out the door. It's referred to as the "*fore and aft method*" in my 1959 St. John Ambulance First Aid book. She had been lying in one position for too long and her limbs were stiff and unmoving, like a butterfly whose wings will not open.

TABLE

Model 44 G 60

You can be a Grade-A Genius if you cook on a kitchen-tested Gurney Range, with EVERY automatic feature to save time, money, talent. With it cooking perfection becomes YOURS! You're *always* At Home On the Range if you're cooking with an even heat Gurney. Ask your dealer about Gurney Ranges. Have beauty in *your* kitchen at low cost. Choose from Gurney coal-and-wood ranges, or gas ranges for Natural, Manufactured or Bottled Gas.

G-30-26N

TABLE

Diane Schoemperlen

The mother slapped the plates down on the table in that way all angry mothers do. The father, folding up his newspaper, pretended not to notice. Or maybe he didn't notice. Maybe he was too busy thinking about other things. About a story he'd just read in the paper about a man who'd murdered his wife and her lover in Toronto (that evil city), and in the photograph the man was being led from the courtroom with a black coat over his head. About the pretty woman in the corner store who had flirted with him when he stopped to buy a treat for his daughter on the way home from work. Maybe he was thinking about fixing himself another rum and Coke.

Or maybe he did notice and just thought all women were like that: furious. Maybe his friends' wives were like that too. Maybe that was what the men talked about in the lunchroom at the paper mill while eating the sandwiches their wives had slapped together the night before. Maybe that was what they laughed about while carefully smoothing and refolding the sheets of wax paper and the little brown bags, returning them to their black lunch pails because if they didn't, there'd be hell to pay at home.

The daughter picked at the foam rubber backing on the yellow plastic placemat and studied the plate plopped in front of her. It was plaid, of all things, brown-and-white plaid. The daughter was mortified. She thought she would die, just *die*, if she had to eat one more meal off these plates at this table with these people.

The table was blue Arborite, speckled with white-and-gold flecks, and it had splayed chrome tubular legs and ridged silver edges. Crumbs and grease had collected between the Arborite and the silver rim. The table pulled apart in the middle where an extension could be inserted for special occasions.

The father, Clarence, dished out the potatoes and the peas. The mother, Esther, slapped a pork chop on each plaid plate. The daughter, Joanna, clenched her teeth and looked at the pork chop on the plaid plate on the yellow placemat on the blue table and thought, as do all people past the age of twelve, how much happier she'd been when she was younger. She had just turned thirteen three weeks before.

She remembered a rainy Saturday when she was six or seven and had spent the whole afternoon beneath this kitchen table, drawing on its underside with her new crayons. Her mother was cooking pork hocks in the big silver pot and she let Joanna colour to her heart's content and she wasn't even mad. Her father was building bookshelves in her bedroom and the circular saw was singing. The whole house was filled with the humid fragrances of boiling meat and cut wood. When Clarence came into the kitchen, there were curls of blond wood tangled in his dark hair like ringlets.

Before that she was even happier. There was the story her mother loved to tell of how Joanna would haul the cookbook drawer out from under her bed (no one ever questioned the rationale of keeping the cookbooks in an old dresser drawer under the little girl's bed) and make up wild and fantastic stories from them. She could not remember but could clearly imagine herself sitting cross-legged on the kitchen floor with a cookbook open in her lap and her mother at the table rolling sweet dough and stamping out cookies with the special silver cutters, and Joanna was saying, "Once upon a time, there was a beautiful mommy," and Esther was laughing and laughing with flour on her nose and white sugar in her wavy black hair. When she sat down on the floor and kissed the little girl's cheek, her hair fell around them like a fragrant curtain.

Joanna's favourite cookbook had been the one with the line drawings of different animals. They said: BEEF, VEAL, PORK.

They did not say: COW, CALF, PIG. Only the LAMB was called by its real name. She knew about Mary and her little lamb, whose fleece was white as snow. She knew about March, which if it came in like a lion, would then go out like a lamb. She did not know yet about sacrifice.

Each drawing was carefully divided into sections labelled in capital letters: CHUCK, RIB, RUMP, LOIN, BRISKET, FATBACK, PICNIC SHOULDER. Only the PORK still had its head, tail, and feet on. The others had stumps instead.

Joanna carefully coloured these diagrams in startling Crayola colours: yellow, red, blue, purple, the LAMB with a turquoise leg, the BEEF with a kelly green rump. It never occurred to her that this was how the animals were butchered. She was so innocent, no wonder she was happier then ...

Now Esther and Clarence were stuffing their mouths, making meaningless dinnertime talk, and Joanna was miserably chewing on a piece of pork chop, chewing and chewing until it was a pulpy chunk of dead white flesh in her throat.

Perhaps she had never been happy. Maybe she was no happier when she was younger than she was now, no happier then than she would ever be. She thought of how her mother always made her rip up the bread for the turkey dressing on Christmas, Easter, and Thanksgiving. Esther would cover the kitchen table with yesterday's newspaper and bring out the huge silver mixing bowl and bags half-full of stale white bread. Then Joanna would perch on the edge of the table and shred the bread into the bowl while Esther complained the whole time that the chunks were too big, the chunks were too small, she was getting crumbs all over the floor, she wasn't making enough, she was making too much, how big did she think that bird was anyway? Then Esther would whisk the full bowl away, sprinkle it with lukewarm water and poultry seasoning, shove whole handfuls into the naked white bird so that her arm disappeared into its bum nearly up to the elbow. By the time the turkey was cooked, Esther was slapping down those plaid plates again, Clarence was asleep or half-drunk, and Joanna thought she would die, just *die*, if she had to eat one more

Christmas, Easter, or Thanksgiving dinner off these plates at this table with these people.

After the turkey there would be pumpkin pie for dessert, a frozen pie crust with canned filling, and Clarence never learned not to say that his mother's pumpkin pie was better than this. Esther, despite the cookbooks under the bed, was not much of a cook.

Tonight there would be vanilla ice cream and canned pears for dessert. Joanna remembered how she used to be allowed to pour a little hot tea over her ice cream and then muck around with it until her bowl was filled with a luscious sweet goop which she spooned carefully into her mouth, and sometimes they would even let her have a second bowl. Of course she was too old for such foolishness now.

Tonight her mother admitted that the pork chops were dry, the mashed potatoes were lumpy, the peas were mushy, and the cucumbers in vinegar and salt were already giving her gas. Clarence agreed with everything she said. He nodded and burped. Esther leapt up and began slamming the dirty dishes into the sink while Clarence ambled towards the living room. (Esther and Clarence called the living room "the front room." They also said "chesterfield" instead of "couch." Joanna was embarrassed. They sounded like farmers or foreigners.) Clarence would sit in there all evening, doing the newspaper crossword puzzle and the cryptogram. Or else he would work on his paint-by-number sets. He did horse heads, seascapes, forest scenes, and gulls in flight. Once he did a pair of nudes: two brown-haired women with nipples the same colour as their hair, smiling lips the same colour as their toenails, each of them holding a blue towel draped carefully to cover their private parts. Esther made Clarence hang the nudes in the garage.

In the kitchen, Joanna dried the dishes and convinced herself that, if she had to eat one more meal in this house at this table with these people, she would never grow up and get free. It never occurred to her to ask Esther what she was always so mad about ...

KITCHEN CREW

Cindy Dean-Morrison

In busy times we'd bring in extra help,
and the fields would sprout extra bodies
needing to be fed.

My mother and I were the kitchen crew.

Breakfast,
    dishes.
    "Run the gas truck out to Bill."
Lunch,
    dishes.
    "Go into town and get that part for the 44."
Supper,
    dishes.
    "Mend these torn overalls."

We cooked, washed, drove, delivered,
from damp dawn till night's crisp blackness,
scrubbing the midnight dishes slowly, quietly,
in the dim, still kitchen
so as not to wake the slumbering workers.

The men piled in at mealtime,
some wore their importance like a John Deere 3010,
others nodded, embarrassed,
hoping not to be noticed;
all slapped dirt off greasy coveralls,
grunted into chairs.

Room only for workers around the table,
my mother and I moved about,
passing buttered carrots, mountains of moist beef,
pouring tea from the old tin pot,
not eating until all others were full.

Once, a bloated salesman arrived at lunch.
At meal's end our stomachs grew excited,
but he smeared the last of the potatoes and gravy
onto his plate, into himself.
"Can't let these go to waste," he said.

SWEET RED PEPPERS

Liz Zetlin

Isn't it funny how so much time passes
before you do the things you promise yourself.
Like show your mother how to roast sweet
red peppers, or ask her if
she's afraid of dying.

Two Septembers have already passed
since I brought her a freezer bag full
of roasted red peppers, part of the bushel
I'd put up that fall. Two Septembers since
she thanked me and asked if I'd show her how.
Two Septembers of packing her freezer
with things I've grown.

So here we are sitting at my kitchen table
in the middle of a neighbourhood where women
make illegal fires to roast cauldrons of peppers
while their men sample this year's batch
of wine. Hands oily with pepper juice,
we hold small knives. Swearing,
we pick off the hot burnt skin. Hell, we agree,
must be when skin will not come loose.
Each has her own method of attack.
She concentrates on the tool, fillet knife
carefully poised, because she knows how easily
a nerve can be severed, especially
around kitchen tables. And me, unrelenting
observer who picks only the ones
whose skins are flayed.

All of a sudden, just as I'm about to ask
if she's afraid of dying, my mother stops
peeling and chopping to caress the scarlet
coloured flesh, *soft as the inside of a thigh*,
she says, in that way she has of filling moments
with joy. Crying out how
good it feels. And I know
she also means this day, this being together,
this celebration of a season completed,
red oil running down our arms, the lilt
in her voice, my question unasked, the time
that will or will not come, no matter
how many promises I make.

Half a Pound of Tea

Maureen Hynes

My mother bought loose tea, tea that came in bricks, like a pound of butter, but as soon as you opened the brick, tore back a corner of the soft foil wrapping and dug a spoon into the black crumbs, it collapsed, spilling curly grains on the green-and-white gingham shelf paper. A dozen times a day she pulled the brick out and replaced it, upended, on the cupboard shelf above the shrieking kettle.

At the end of a long rainy Saturday, five o'clock and the magic show on Channel 4 over, my sister and I fighting about a box of animal crackers or my paper dolls, the living room upended and spilling like the brick of tea, my mother stood at the stove, groaning *Oh, my nerves* into the steam of the macaroni pot. She'd get a glinty look in her eye and start humming the cheery melody, and then later, giving us a bath, when we were still wild and splashing, she'd lean her face close to ours and sing the whole song:

> *This is the day they give babies away*
> *With half a pound of tea*
> *If you know any ladies who want any babies*
> *Send them all to me.*

It was the same kind of tune as *If you go down to the woods today*, the kind that bounced and burrowed in your head. So that the next day, we would find ourselves humming the song into our doll carriages, to our teddy bears, over the rubber houses we were building with our Mini-brix, and we'd stop, wondering if all the mothers sang this song. It was like the nursery rhyme, *down come baby, cradle and all*—here's how to kill your baby, but somehow the nursery rhyme felt like ours, it wasn't the mothers' song. Is that what all the mothers wanted, to give their babies away?

It was worse than when she'd cry out, exasperated, *I'm going to run away with the tinkers,* and I'd say, *Hah, they don't have tinkers in Canada.* If she just hummed the tune, we'd still talk back, but it troubled us later, it worked all right. The fear. Not that she'd give us away now, but that she wished she *had* given us away, and her wishes would sometimes come traipsing down the street, back home after working out of town for a couple of months, back to our house, for a nice long afternoon visit, for a pot of tea with her.

Advice from My Mother Concerning Root Vegetables

Marilynn Rudi

Beets
You can cook and eat the tender greens
in summer. Steam lightly and season
with butter, salt and pepper. Serve to your
husband with cold sliced tongue
and sharp mustard.
You can wait till fall
and eat the firm red roots.
Boil with skins on, for the colour
bleeds. When fully cooked,
the shiny bulb slips easily from its skin.
Protect your hands, or you'll look like a butcher.
Pickled beets are nice and last all winter.
Your grandfather loved your granny's beets
and horseradish. I've heard tell they make
sugar out of beets, but I've never tried it.

Turnips
She's the queen of the fall, a pale yellow-skinned
lass with a purple crown. Peel and cube her flesh,
boil and mash. Turns golden yellow. Add a dollop
of butter; my, how fine! The smaller the turnip,
the sweeter. Throw them into any soup or stew
you've got simmering on the stove.
You can eat them raw, cut into strips;
flavour's peppery and crisp.
My granny said they used to hollow
them and use the rinds as lanterns.

Parsnips
Look just like carrots, only creamy white.
Use a peeler to scrape the skin, slice and boil.
They mash up smooth as potatoes though drier.
One of the sweetest of the roots but with a spicy nip.
Mighty tasty with roasted joints of meat. For heaven's sake,
don't go confusing them with cow parsnip—
that's a yellow-flowered weed.

Carrots
What's a kitchen without 'em? Necessary as
salt and pepper. Tasty raw, boiled, glazed, roasted,
simmered, stewed or sauced. Paired with beef,
potatoes, peas: a marriage made in heaven.
Don't choose any with green bits—
they're bitter. Carrots get sweeter as they cook.
Did you know back when sugar was hard to come by,
they used mashed carrots in cakes and puddings?
Wild carrots are called Queen Anne's Lace. Their roots
are spindly red things, not much eating there.
In my time, I've found a few carrots
that look for all the world
like a man with two legs!
Oh, don't worry, they didn't shriek
as I plucked them from the earth.

Discontinued China Pattern

Myrna Garanis

The antiques mall is a hall of temptation for those over-tuned
to the past. I succumb to a kitchen weigh scale that measures
in pounds. Fall for its classic clean white lines,
its Buddha ability to stand and wait.

I am bowled over by the grand array of gold-rimmed, fine bone
china. Rows of the discontinued. My mother's is there: American
Beauty Rose, acquired long after her wedding, long after war
secured luxury money. Pickle dish, handled candy tray, salt
and pepper, sides. She never managed dinner plates,
and was satisfied with cup-by-cup accretion.

Silver Birch. Blossom Time, Old Country Roses. Her sisters' cabinets
groaned with completed settings plus silver plate parked in velour-
lined chests. My mother's Royal Albert fit on one unreachable shelf.
Dusted for rare afternoon guests, gold rims unworn. Grandsons
wrapped and removed her American Beauty for numerous
relocations, frailty on their minds.

Here in the mall of abandoned plates and forks, my chance to swell
her modest collection. Six salad plates in fine condition. If I say
the word, they'll throw in a dainties dish. I turn away, yield

to her years of gathering slow.

A Taste of Lemon

Rosemary Clewes

Saturday mornings mother washed my hair.
I knelt, knees doubled on the high stool,
                                    head tipped
into the basin: her fingers knowing all the tender places,
cast and slope of my crown,
                        temple hollows.

I gulped air between cupfuls   dowsing soapy drifts
    washcloth pressed
                      pixelated light waves chasing stars
    behind my eyes
                suds whispering staticky nothings
as I imagined clouds would if they could talk.

My mother always trickled fresh lemon at the end,
then rinsed. Its taste made me lick my lips like a cuddled puppy.
She towelled and combed.
                "Ohooo," I moaned, "you're hurting me,"
but my hair dried to fly-away-fineness. I listened,
eyes half-closed to the crackling air, her hands gathering,
tightening a wide ribbon's rustling loops over my right ear.

                I reach up to caress the shine, the taffeta bow.
My first line of poetry pops out before I know it.
Pleased, I profess my hair is crisp as bacon.

ROYAL JELLY

Marilyn Gear Pilling

We bathed in succession in the same water,
me first, little brother, baby sister, mother,
father last. The order always the same,
the water clean and warm when I had my
bath, grey and tepid by the time
our father had his.
       Once, I was remembering
this aloud, telling the story to my teenage
daughters in the presence of my mother.
My daughters squealed *Gross,*
one of them threw herself on the carpet
and windmilled her extremities, a white-limbed
octopus of distaste.
I said that it was strange
that I'd always gone first and my mother
said, *Oh no oh no not strange at all*
we always catered to you, you
were the Queen Bee in that household.
This was in the days when such truths offended
me, and I flushed and denied it
at which the octopus rose from the rug,
swept her mimicking self
across the room in a way that was
royal highnessy and unmistakably
me, and my mother shook like cubed Jell-O
at a family reunion, she and my daughters
laughed so hard their canines shone
and I wanted to kill them all.

33

    That's as long ago
now as the serial bathing was then
and of course I'd give every jar of royal jelly
in the hive to see that Jell-O on the picnic table
again, how the faces of those ruby cubes
juggled the light.

WHAT I DIDN'T KNOW THEN

Liz Zetlin

When I was four, night-flowered in flannel,
I didn't know why my mom stopped reading
just after: "When I was one/I had just begun."
She sobbed into silence then spoke:
> *thinking of my first born*
> *who died when he was one.*

I remember wondering how she could miss
someone that little. Maybe I even
said the thought out loud.
How long it takes to forgive
all my callous little selves.

At the age of five I didn't know why she
let me stay up late to be the three witches
with her Shakespeare-reading friends.
Double, double toil and trouble
Fire burn, and caldron bubble
When my own words began to boil
I knew why words aloud held
such power.

At six I didn't know why she slapped me
(that one and only time) when I answered
"only if it's fresh squeezed" to our host
asking if I would like some orange juice.
I thought that showed such good taste.

At eleven I didn't know why she sent me away
on Saturday mornings to chant *baruch 'atoi adonai,*
eluhaenu meloch olum. I didn't know, by hearing
ritual language up close, she hoped there would be
no mystery in the swaying of the robe, the unrolling
of the parchment scroll, the repeated prayers,

the lighting of candles. She inoculated me
in small doses.

I didn't know why she had her own ritual movements.
Barely able to see above the steering wheel, driving
me across town to grade nine, the year Norfolk closed
its public schools rather than integrate, she gripped
the wheel with both hands, her right thumb
working itself free. The thumb jerked up and down
as she drove, as she talked about shoes dyed to match,
as we sat silent. I prayed my friends wouldn't notice
this only sign she gave me then, a secret message
even the sender couldn't decode.

Much later I knew I was witnessing the insides
of my mother, dancing to an erratic rhythm, almost
as though the thumb didn't belong to her, demanding
its rightful place, even if only at the very end of her.

Back then, all I wanted was to grab my mother's thumb,
stop it from jerking, force its energy
up her arm, across her shoulder into
her throat, where it would leap into voice.
How I needed that voice to tell me
what possessed her so
and what there was (or could be)
to put my faith in.

A few years before she died she told me
about the first time she tried to draw.
I was the age she was then at the kitchen table,
late in her forties, when she picked up a felt pen,
as if for the first time. The pressure familiar
against her writer's bump. But instead of a rush
of vowels and consonants, she felt a line
flow out of her.

Urgent and seismic the lines began.
So fine they could record each moment
of doubt. So thick they could hold all
the tears she had ever cried. Silk threads
from a spider's centre, they looped
and swirled, knowing
she was meant to do this.

All I knew then (sometime in my thirteenth year)
when I saw her lines start to flow
was her thumb had stopped jerking.

After she died, early in her eighties,
her kitchen table became the place
where I began to unravel knotted threads.
And sometimes, just before I turn out the light,
I see her sitting there. She dips a Chinese brush
into a bowl of water, smoothes it over a stick
of black ink onto fresh white paper.
She and the ink breathe together.
I hold my breath as I watch
these strands of faith dissolving
in the flow of tinted water
as they become buttery strokes of oil,
polymers of acrylic, pieces of stone
and copper, microchips and coral,
a fine spray painted mist.

I didn't know then the doctors would suspect
those sprayed dots of colour
made the shadows on her lungs.

Or that those colours
would run through her ashes, fine
as painted sand.

HAPPY AND LUCKY

Judy Fong Bates

My mother, Fong Yet Lan, once told me her life was like a table that had been sawn in two: one half had stayed in China, the other half had been sent to Canada. I was nine, perhaps ten, when she told me this. And ever since, I have remembered the image of those two collapsed pieces of table. In my child's mind, I had imbued them with feelings; I pictured them like a Disney cartoon, both sad and comical, each failing miserably to stand upright. I yearned to bring those two stranded parts together.

In the elementary school where I attended grade five, there was a roll-down map of the world hanging over a section of the blackboard. My teacher took a pencil and made a dot near the tip of Lake Ontario that jutted out over Lake Erie. That was where we lived. Acton, Ontario, she said. But my classmates weren't paying attention; they were busy sneaking glances out the window at the falling snow. It was almost recess, and everyone was eager to put on their winter coats and boots and run outside to play. Everyone except me. While they got ready, I walked up to the map, mesmerized by this large, pink country and the tiny, black dot that represented our town. I put my finger on it, then traced up to the top of Lake Superior, across the Prairies, over the Rockies and then over the blue Pacific Ocean. I felt a knot of desperation tightening in the pit of my stomach; so much land, so much water separating our small town from the south of China, where, I had been told, it never snowed. The distance felt insurmountable. How would my mother ever bring the two halves of her table together?

We languished in Hong Kong for only two years, but in my hazy remembrance the time feels longer, another lifetime belonging to someone else. I have no memory of Doon living with us, and yet I know he did. He was in his late teens and spent his days exploring the city on his own and with other young relatives who were waiting to emigrate. That period of my life has left me with a vague but persistent impression of that city's excitement, a memory of constantly turning my head and looking, my mother holding me by the wrist while we walked along congested sidewalks and through outdoor markets swarming with people. Often, by the end of the day, I was a sullen child. My legs ached as I dragged my feet and followed my mother from temple to temple, walking among massive stone statues of gods, staring up at their silent faces, the air smoky and fragrant with incense, my mother making offerings, her hands clasped in prayer.

My mother clenched my hand inside hers while I struggled to keep up as we pushed our way through another noisy market until she reached a particular fortuneteller. Ming Nee and I stood on either side of our mother and watched the man toss sticks into the air. He then read them after they landed on a smooth, wooden table. Once he was finished, we rushed to another clairvoyant, who released a small, white bird to choose a tiny square of folded paper with black writing on it. The writing would be interpreted by the clairvoyant, who then told my mother its meaning. I waited, holding my breath with anticipation, but hoping for what? Both times my mother handed over money, never smiling. She grabbed my hand and pushed her way back through the crowds, Ming Nee following behind. Whatever it was my mother was told that day she never shared with me.

Not long after our arrival, we started to visit a family with four daughters who seemed about the same age as Ming Nee. They were from our home village and we called the mother Auntie. After my mother and I left Hong Kong, Ming Nee would live with them. She was not my father's daughter and would have to endure another three long years for our mother to attain Canadian citizenship in order to sponsor her immigration.

Then one day my mother purchased a large, hard-sided suitcase with metal clasps, and without being told, I knew that our life in Hong Kong was about to end. I watched as she filled it with dried herbal medicines; a warm, brown woolen blanket with a shiny satin binding; new clothes for me, yards of fabric; and skeins of wool. She had heard that Canada was a cold country, where the people were large, and that it would be hard for her to find clothes to fit her small frame. My mother consulted a tailor and had a navy-blue travel suit made, and she went to a beauty salon, where someone permed her hair into a nest of tight curls. All these things my mother did in preparation for our journey across the Pacific. She approached her chores methodically and without complaint. But she never smiled. On the day we left Hong Kong, she wore her new suit and a gold necklace with a heart-shaped pendant that had the word HAPPY embossed on it. I wore a gold bracelet with the letters L-U-C-K-Y linked in a chain. At the time they were only a collection of *lo fon* ABCs.

When we left for the airport in Hong Kong, my mother wept, not letting go of Ming Nee until we had to board the airplane. A tall *lo fon* stewardess ushered us into line; my mother held my hand the entire time, but her head was turned away from me. She was staring at her oldest daughter, who remained on the other side of the gate, tears streaming down her face, shoulders heaving. We stood to the side for a few moments, allowing other passengers to embark. Auntie, who had been waiting beside Ming Nee, finally led her away, and my mother and I walked through the portal. I looked up and saw my mother's face all twisted. She gripped my hand even tighter. It wasn't until I was an adult with children of my own that I began to have a real understanding of the anguish my mother must have been feeling; she was leaving behind her thirteen-year-old daughter.

My mother never touched any of the food the flight attendants brought. But for me it was an adventure, and when I first tasted tiny cubes of soft fruit floating in a small bowl of clear, sugary syrup, I thought it was delicious. There were other Chinese women on the airplane, some of whom seemed to be about my mother's age. And, like my mother, they were about to join husbands from whom they had been separated for many years. But there was one woman who I could tell was younger. Her complexion was smooth, and there was a nervousness about her. She reminded me of Ming Nee and was probably not much older. My mother said she was a mail-order bride, that she would marry her husband once she arrived. I noticed that all the women, even the mail-order bride, had their hair permed into curls, just like my mother, and that every one of them was wearing gold necklaces, bracelets and earrings.

It was night when the plane landed in Vancouver. I remember only bright-coloured lights against a dark sky. A smiling Chinese man took a group of us on a bus, first to a hotel and then to a restaurant, where my mother ate almost nothing. The next day, we boarded another flight. This time there were fewer Chinese people on the airplane. Everybody was going to a big city, my mother told me. We were the only ones bound for a hand laundry in a small town.

PLAY SCHOOL

Play School

Betsy Struthers

Some days our mother calls us Holy Terrors. We use the bathmat to toboggan down the stairs, we have pillow fights in bedrooms, we are taunted by Doris's gang into games of Red Rover and Fox and Goose, games that turn into tears and someone stomping home, threatening to tell on all of us.

Other days we loll about the living room, Like Lumps according to our mother, listening to the radio, *Secret Storm* and *The Guiding Light*. The big kids have gone back to school and our mother Will Not let us play in the long back yards alone. The sow on Buddy's father's farm has escaped from her pen twice and come to root potatoes from our garden. Our mother herds us all indoors and yells at Buddy's mother on the phone to come and fetch it back before it does Something We Will All Regret. Our mother has read that pigs ate babies in the days when farmers and their animals shared quarters and she is afraid for us though we say we are *not* babies and not even old Shep, the collie, is allowed inside Buddy's house. Still, we all stand together and watch from our mother's bedroom window as Buddy's mother, in apron and rubber boots, whacks the sow with a broom and Shep chases it back across the fence line out of sight.

If only there were a kindergarten here, our mother sighs to our father. (We are lying on the floor in the upstairs hall, ears pressed to the register.) *Why don't you start one?* he says.

Now in the morning, after the fathers and the older kids have left and breakfast is cleared away, our gang gathers in the sunporch. Our father has built a long table with long benches, room enough for all of us to sit together. Our mother has boxes of crayons and piles of paper from our father's business, with typing on one side and blank on the other, perfect for colouring. She sits in the wicker rocking chair, reading us stories. Our favourites are Pooh (though this makes us giggle) and The Jungle Book, Mother Goose and Robert Louis Stevenson. How we love his name! One of us makes up a rhyme perfect for hop-scotch:

> Ro—bert Lou—ie Ste—ven—son
> Went to bed with his waistcoat—on
> Died at seven
> Went to Heaven
> Now he's got his ha—lo—on.

We cover old light bulbs with layers of newspaper and flour-and-water paste and, when they are dried, we paint them and crack them on the edge of the table to break the glass inside. *Maracas*, our mother calls them. Buddy's mother brings over an old sleigh harness and our mother cuts it into pieces we can shake to make jingle bells. Marilyn's father lends a real snare drum. Our mother makes us take turns putting its red belt around our waists. Whoever is drummer must match the stamping of our feet with taps on its round white face.

We bundle into our coats and outdoor shoes and mittens. One of us is given the flag to carry, a flutter of red at the end of a broomstick, one of us the drum, all of us have our maracas and bells. We march out the sunporch door, along the path to the driveway, down the drive to the back door, through the kitchen and the hall back to the sunporch. We sing *God Save the Queen* while the flag waves and the drum drums. Sometimes we parade three or even four times while our mother calls out "left, right, left." She was a Sergeant in the War, and, although she mostly worked in an office, she had Done Her Duty and she knows a Proper March when she sees one.

Doris tags along with the parade, at least as far as the back door. Her mother has asked that she join the play school, but our mother has said there is No More Room. To our father, she said, *that's one more than I Can Handle*. We tell Doris to stay off our property, so now she and her gang skulk on the roadside and make up dirty words to go with our song. We ignore them. The snow is melting and we time our splashing through puddles to the beat of the drum. Our mother only sighs and mops the hall behind us.

We are planning an Easter Concert. All the mothers will be invited and we will learn special songs for our parade: *Peter Cottontail* and *In My Easter Bonnet*. We make our bonnets out of paper plates decorated with tissue flowers and ribbons and bows. Our mother has taught us all to tie our shoes and now we practice and practice making bows to get the knot under our chins just right, the loops wide and floppy.

Our mothers are dressed in their shiniest dresses and carry purses that they place carefully under the chairs lined up in the dining room. We are all in our Sunday clothes, skirts and corduroys and stiff white shirts. Before the parade, we are to play quietly in the front yard while our mothers view the Exhibition of artwork taped to the sunroom windows. Then, while they settle with their cups of tea, we will don our bonnets and get our orchestra ready.

Doris is in the ditch where the meltwater has made a bed of clay. *Look at you guys*, she jeers, *you look like a bunch of fairies*. Her gang choruses after her, *Fairies-airies*. They pick up gobs of clay and throw them in our direction. Soon we are all in the ditch, fighting.

A car horn beeps, a car turns into our drive. A blue car, a strange car, in the middle of the day when all the fathers are away at work. We fall apart and stand, smeared and dripping, staring. A very tall, very thin woman in a narrow black suit gets out of the car. She wears a hat with a veil tucked under its rim and carries a clipboard in white-gloved hands. She has very red lips. She snorts at the sight of us, a sound, we decide later, just like the sow makes when she noses out a rotten potato.

The mothers come to the door. The Clipboard Woman says *I understand you are running some kind of school here. Who is the teacher? May I see your certificate?*

After the blue car leaves and the other mothers leave, we find our mother sitting in the living room, the radio not on, her hands folded in her lap so tightly we can see the bones of her knuckles. She says, *Please go out and play quietly. I have a Splitting Headache.*

We sit under the silver poplar in the back yard. One of us has picked a handful of chives and we share them, sucking on the stems. Buddy says that he heard his mother tell Jill's mother that Doris's mother ratted to the school board, because our mother would not let Doris join the school. Buddy's mother said the play school is Finished. We all say that we hate Doris and that she will never be our friend. We join hands in a circle and raise them high and lower them, three times. Death to Doris, we say. We link our pinky fingers. One for All. We press our palms flat, each to each. All for One.

Marilyn's mother has taken away the drum and Buddy's mother the jingle bells. Still, we have our maracas and our bonnets. We enter the sunporch silently and put them on, we stand in a line from shortest to tallest, Buddy at the front holding the flag though we are not going to sing the Queen song. Still, a parade needs a flag, we are all agreed. One of us begins. *Here comes Peter Cottontail.* We march in step down the hall through the kitchen, past the empty line of chairs in the dining room, into the living room. Our mother is on her knees, hugging us. *Oh you kids*, she says.

Afterwards it is spring and the sow is too busy with her piglets to think of the garden. Then it is summer and then September and we are all going to grade one. Our mother stands in the sunporch door, waving and waving. Every time we turn around, she is still there. *Good-bye*, she cries. *So long.*

ASSEMBLY LINE

Alice Major

Children restless in a wriggled line
beside the boot-to-bonnet hubbub of buses.
A hopscotch of thick kilts.
Each child issued with a clock-shaped badge
cut from coloured construction paper
and pinned to woolly Fair-Isle jumpers.

The children of a thousand employees
in the Westclox factory
offered this junket up to Kelvin Hall
to see the circus.
Her two girls among them, the eldest
disappointed in the dull brown
of the badge assigned to her.

Mary waved goodbye, turned to her shift—
the work of taking things apart, clock movements
ill-made on the plant's brand-new assembly line
that constructed ten thousand clocks a week.
Her quick fingers unscrewed face plates
stamped "Made in Scotland," tossed
steel wheels into boxes for re-use.
Minute hands by the hour.

The post-war blast of production
made cheap time a priority—alarms and chimes
needed for conveying workers to their shifts.
The old clocks all run down by war.
Mary's pay cheque put aside each week
to help afford their passage overseas,
to slip this particular chain
of being, this conveyor going
to a dull brown destination.

While the children—that bright bulge
of post-war assembly—
watched the sparkling ballerinas
go round and round the ring
balanced on their silver-backed horses,
while the clowns flipped themselves
through linked hoops, and the elephants
shuffled their trunk-to-tail train.

Then looked round for their clock-colour buddies,
were instructed to take hands, form chains
climb back aboard their line
of puffing buses.

FAMILIAR BLUE COAT

Joanne Page

Shoosta lamagoosta Father sings in the tub reading *The New Yorker* and listening to the Yankees on a red plastic radio that Mother yells at him to not touch, or the light switch, for fear of electrocution yet he hears her not, as he has slipped into his other bathroom song done in a Daffy Duck voice *O what a bunch of ducks on the lake today* which the children favour over the Elmer Fudd that makes him sound like his cousin, the Prime Minister, whom they are taught to regard with some familiarity, though they have never met, but know well his brother who comes to watch hockey and talks right through the exciting bits, driving everyone to hint he might want to get his galoshes on and hurry home to Mother, pronounced Annie-the-Phoner by the lily grandmother as she sets the talking telephone down, and smiles. Mother has a decided taste for Yankee politics, as it happens, and works herself into a lather over Joseph McCarthy, only surpassed by her loathing of J. Edgar the Hoover, both of whom she takes to audible task, standing arms akimbo, before our new Motorola TV, that also shows Howdy Doody with his forty-eight russet freckles, one for each state of the Union across the Great Lake. Not much of a cook, the mother sticks to pressure cooker stew, Spanish rice, and canned peas, all to be consumed in the dining room, with due decorum, which suffers a setback when she begins to serve salad with an Italian dressing that leaves Thousand Island in the lurch, and so appeals to the dad that he takes to lifting the bowl, both eyes on his wife, and draining it dry, a little rebellion not lost on anyone.

The red-headed girl overhears her mother on the phone explaining how sorry she is that her daughter invited all of Miss Sharp's grade two class to her house Friday after school for a birthday party, as the actual date is not Friday, but six months hence, in early spring, plain echo to the time she came home from school for lunch the day King George died and declared that it was she who lowered the flag while the whole school watched at recess, completely failing to shock her mother, even surprise her, with the outlandishness of the boldfaced lie. Unlike other mothers on the block, headquarters is not the stove. She prefers the den with its phone, ashtray, stack of library books, and west window overlooking the yard and, though she does not care to cook, will take a full week to brew up a marathon batch of chili sauce, smelling up their school coats and even clothes hung upstairs in closets. Neither does she sew, though she labours through a Singer course one winter and turns out what she calls serviceable skirts in matching tweed for each of them, thereafter the sewing machine on one end of the dining room table until she gives it away. That afternoon after Old Dick has come to visit and gone, she explains he began with horses and never could manage cars, which was a disadvantage for a chauffeur, so she and her brothers put him in back and drove themselves to school. On the other hand he patched, which came in handy going to Caledon, reversing up The Mountain on Highway Ten, three or four flats in a one-way trip to the farm where the horses no longer grazed and Orange Crush crates filled the room with the party line phone. The mother applies scarlet polish to her nails one hand at a time then blows them dry, a little freshening, as they are going to The Club to watch the red-haired girl's winter carnival, where she will be picked at the last minute to give a bouquet to Barbara Ann Scott, and skating towards her, she will trip and fall flat on her face to a collective groan, then cheer from the crowd, as the star rights her so they can glide together, to a perky skaters' waltz, around the entire pad of ice, then to the edge, with a spraying stop, where she's delivered to the scarlet-tipped hands of the smiling mother, who wraps her in the familiar blue coat, and says: *How great, dear, did you plan it?*

THE SOUR RED CHERRIES

Marilyn Gear Pilling

came ripe in July and their last week
on the tree was war.
My mother was out there at dawn every morning
in her long white night-
gown, finger on the trigger,
one eye closed, mouth under her moustache
pressed tight. When she pulled
the trigger the unholy
racket scattered starlings and robins all over the sky,
caused the dog to lay his ears flat
to his head and howl, and the bay yearling
to thud to the back fence.

After breakfast, my aunt handed the rifle
to my sister, scrubbed the sleepers from our eyes
and sent us to start our shift on two kitchen chairs
outside, guarding the cherries.
Marie's method was a cavalier fire
at the sky, rifle askew at arm's
length, pointed in any old
direction. We laughed behind our hands
when our mother came out to demonstrate her squint,
her careful aim; the rifle was a toy, its only ammunition
the eschatological intensity of its explosion

Many years later, in winter, our mother died with one
cherry pie in the freezer. Marie and I
thawed the pie; while it warmed, we stood at the pantry
window, looked out at the shrouded bones
of tree, talked of searching for the rifle,
firing one last salute. Instead, we sat up to the worn oilcloth
and ate half the pie each. Every bite exploded
sweet-sour summer in our mouths
and we scraped and scraped
our pink-flowered plates with our forks 'til they shrieked,
then stuck out our tongues and licked and licked
'til the china was wet with happiness.

At the Corner of Sunset and Virginia

Jane Munro

In the mid-Fifties, Mrs. Mitchell, Mrs. Piercy, Mrs. Handy, Mrs. Allen, Mrs. Johnson, and my mother, Mrs. Southwell, lived within hailing distance of one another at the corner of Sunset Boulevard and Virginia Crescent. Unlike the other mothers, mine went out the door after breakfast, got into her Triumph Mayflower, and drove herself to work.

In those days, married women did not take jobs away from men, and very few owned cars. But, when my father was building our house and they desperately needed money, Mom went back to substituting. She was soon hired as a full-time teacher. Many schools were so full they'd gone on swing shifts; Mom had taught for twelve years as a single woman, and her principal decided that— married or not—she was an essential addition to his staff. Later, she became one of the first girls' counsellors in North Vancouver. She earned more than Dad and became the sustaining bread-winner for the family. Pretending this was a temporary anomaly, she signed each of her pay cheques over to him.

And, she apologized to me for her shortcomings: dowdiness (she wore size sixteen dresses and twisted her salt-and-pepper hair up in a roll), being older than the other mothers, and being gone all day.

Even while I was in elementary school, I figured her job sounded a lot more interesting than housework, and announced that I did not intend to be a stay-at-home wife.

"You're wrong!" she insisted. "A woman's greatest fulfillment comes in her role as a wife and mother."

I was dubious: she obviously loved her work and was good at it. I listened to her stories about the problems she faced and the creative solutions she devised to resolve them. Her students thrived and her colleagues became friends. She was promoted. She was praised. I was proud of her and wanted to do just as well myself.

I told her I didn't think much of marriage, and wasn't sure about having children. Realizing that talk alone wasn't going to change my mind, she embarked on a campaign to provide me with appropriate mentors: proper, stay-at-home moms.

∽

Mrs. Mitchell was wearing shorts when she opened the front door. I had never seen legs like hers in real life, only on billboards. Maybe she'd forgotten I was coming. I could look through her house and out the back door to a patch of sunny grass. She toed on a pair of slippers and led me into her kitchen. A fancy magazine, folded open to a photograph of a twelve-layered prune cake, lay on the counter. A cake without icing.

"It's our anniversary," she explained. "I've never made this before but thought it would be fun."

Her white shorts ended in neat little cuffs at the top of her thighs. She had a band of elasticized, bubbly, yellow fabric on her top that stayed up without straps.

I could tell this wasn't going to turn out the way Mom imagined.

When Mrs. Mitchell had come to our house for her "welcome-to-the-neighbourhood" tea, she'd worn a full-skirted shirtwaist and balanced her baby son on her knee. She'd tilted her head back and laughed at Mom's stories. It turned out Mrs. Mitchell had a degree in Home Economics and her husband was a coach at the university. After the others left, Mom fixed Fran, as she'd taken to calling her, with her bright blue gaze and asked her to teach me how to make pastry, something Mom readily admitted she couldn't do herself. They set a date. When the time came, Mom made me scrub my hands, change into a clean blouse, and go knock on Mrs. Mitchell's door.

All the time we were cooking, Mrs. Mitchell left David in the middle of a low table on casters with a hole cut in the middle and a seat inserted. His legs were too short to propel himself around the room so he mostly just dangled there.

Mrs. Mitchell got me to squeeze the pits out of the prunes and squish them together in a pulp. She baked the dough in round cake tins and split the disks. We worked together on stacking and filling. The layers turned out to be different sizes and thicknesses. We tried to distribute the filling evenly, but the stack grew precarious and looked messier than the picture accompanying the recipe. She set it proudly on her sideboard.

I was afraid prune gunk would squirt out and the layers would skid apart when she cut into it, but she told me a few days later that Mr. Mitchell thought her surprise cake was delicious, and they'd laughed a lot. She apologized for not saving a slice for me. I told her that was okay.

I was visiting her because Mom had sent me back to ask for the promised pastry lesson. Mrs. Mitchell was lying on a lounge chair in her back yard. She'd left the front and back doors wide open and had hollered to me to come on through. It was a little odd to visit with her while she was lying down. She shaded her eyes with one hand so she could see me while we chatted. David was in his play pen on the patio.

A week later, I carried my first apple pie across the street and into our house. I got more unconditional praise for that pie than for anything else I ever did.

Mom had actually begun her campaign with Mrs. Piercy, who lived in the house with the butterfly-wing roof at the end of our spur road. She'd insisted I knock on Mrs. Piercy's door and ask if I might help her with Nicole and Mark.

Mrs. Piercy's living room had plate glass windows from floor to ceiling. Its roof flew up steeply making space for another floor beyond the fireplace. Mr. Piercy had his piano up there.

Sometimes Mrs. Piercy let me sit in one of her interesting canvas chairs and give Mark a bottle. There were architectural magazines and books of abstract paintings on the coffee table. A mobile light fixture floated over the dining table.

Mrs. Piercy asked me to call her Marge. She kept a pitcher of orange juice in her refrigerator and, mid-morning, would serve it in tumblers with heavy bottoms and thin top rims. We drank the orange juice while sitting on high black stools at her kitchen bar. Mom cut oranges into quarters for us at breakfast, but she considered juice wasteful.

One day, Marge invited me into the bedroom she'd painted blue for Mark. He was still sleeping in the bassinette in Mr. and Mrs. Piercy's bedroom, but outgrowing it. She went through a rigamarole of consulting me about what a baby might like to look at. I found this an interesting question. We talked for quite a while. Nicky played at our feet. But then it turned out that Marge had already bought a set of train decals in the paint store, and knew exactly where she wanted to put them.

One evening, a few months later, Mr. Piercy came over after supper. He and my parents closed the living room door and talked for a long time. Mom delivered the verdict while we were washing dishes. Marge was in hospital with TB, which was contagious, so I needed to get tested.

Marge's sister came from Toronto to help with the family. Sometimes I'd see Marge walking in her garden and wave, but I wasn't allowed to get close enough to talk. Then, Mr. Piercy was transferred and they moved back to Ontario.

My skin would redden when we got our TB patch tests at school, and I'd be sent for a chest X-ray. I'd think of Marge in her butterfly-wing house: a prize-winning design Mr. Piercy had fallen in love with at a world's fair.

∽

Mrs. Handy was Leanna's mom. Leanna was five years older than I was and well-mannered. The Handys lived next door to us on Sunset. Mrs. Handy never smiled, but under Leanna's bed there was a carton of comic books—*Super Man* and *Archie* and *Little Lulu*—all banned at my house. If I knocked on the back door while they were eating, Mrs. Handy would tell me to make myself at home and wait in Leanna's bedroom. Luckily, Leanna was a slow eater and Mrs. Handy kept her well-supplied with new comic books.

Mrs. Handy's back yard was given over to a flourishing vegetable garden she kept as tidy as her house. One section was filled with rows of raspberries which Leanna and I helped pick. Raspberries were Mom's favourite fruit—she was pleased when I'd bring some home and compliment Mrs. Handy on her green thumb.

Mrs. Handy wore a house dress under a full-length, bibbed, white apron whether she was in gumboots and digging the garden, down on her knees weeding, or ironing in the kitchen. Mom occasionally tied on a shorter apron when she cooked, but she made hers from remnants and trimmed them with rickrack. Like Mrs. Handy, she always wore dresses. This set them apart from the younger mothers.

When Mrs. Handy came to our house with a basin of peas, she entered by the side door. It was closest to her yard but awkward to open because Dad's skill saw sat behind it. She'd ask Mom how she coped with the dust, wonder if she really liked living on a cement slab, offer her cucumbers if she was going to make dills, and murmur, while shaking her head, that she had no idea how she managed. Mom and Mrs. Handy did not use first names. Mom showed me how to shell the peas, but observed it was quicker to open a tin.

Sometimes Leanna let me climb into their Austin when it was parked inside the closed-door garage, and we'd pretend we were driving. This was something else Mom didn't know about. She said playing in cars was dangerous.

⌒

When it got hot, Mrs. Allen set up her rotating sprinkler and let all the kids in the neighbourhood run through it. Mr. Allen played the trumpet. We'd pester until he came out and blared away on it from the back step. Mrs. Allen would give us Kool-Aid in paper cups. We'd stick out green or purple tongues at one another. In the winter, Mrs. Allen would invite us indoors to play in their basement. When they got a TV set, she allowed kids to sit on the couch in their living room and watch.

Mom organized it so I would baby-sit for Mrs. Allen. I got paid 25 cents an hour. She explained: "If there's any problem, we'll be right across the street." Of course, I watched TV all evening and Mrs. Allen told me to help myself to snacks. There were things in her cupboards—like potato chips—that Mom never bought.

Mrs. Johnson's back yard was continuous with Mrs. Allen's; we could run back and forth between them until Mr. Johnson built a fence.

Mrs. Johnson went shopping in the States. Once she came back with a six-year-old boy who was her daughter's uncle. He lived with them until she had another little girl and Mr. Johnson said they needed the bedroom and sent the uncle away.

Each of her daughters could invite one friend into the house at a time. Someone had to leave before another kid entered. They wore nail polish and had dolls in costumes on their bedroom shelves. Mom got me baby-sitting for them, too.

Another time Mrs. Johnson came back from the States with hula-hoops. She taught us how to twirl them. I'd go over after school to practice with her and we'd compete to see who could keep the hoop spinning the longest. When she got tired and quit, she'd offer me a glass of Coke.

∞

Until Mom got her boxy black Triumph Mayflower, she behaved as if she didn't have a license. Dad would take her places or she'd walk. I never saw her drive his green Ford.

When I was six and Dad took her to the hospital so my sister could be born, it was my job to get the coin purse from her top drawer, take my four-year-old brother by the hand, catch the interurban tram to Main and Hastings, get a city bus to the Bay, wait for a West Van blue bus and ride on it to the end of the line, then walk the mile and a half up hill to our friends' house where we'd have macaroni and cheese for lunch and stay the night. This was before we moved to Sunset Boulevard. That night we slept in our underwear on two wing chairs pushed together to make a boat, my brother's head on the seat of one and mine on the other. We had to climb over the arms. When Dad arrived, he slept on the chesterfield.

Mom loved to give parties. I liked to get her to demonstrate "levitation." For this, she needed three straight chairs, six helpers, and a subject. We'd take turns. You lay rigidly across the chairs. The helpers lined up on either side, rather like pall bearers, put their forefingers together and inserted these under your shoulders, hips and knees. With Mom leading, we synchronized our breathing. On the third exhalation all six lifted their arms aloft and you floated up—levitated. By magic.

Mom was one of four graduates from her south Vancouver high school class who went on to university. In the summers she found work berry picking, cleaning cabins, waiting on tables. At some point she discovered she could earn money drawing pen and ink silhouettes—girls in full skirts eating cherries, girls dancing with lacy shawls floating out behind them—which she sold through Birk's jewellery store downtown.

After she'd been teaching for a while, she went off to Columbia University in New York to become a graduate student in Psychology. That ended at Christmas when her mother got sick and insisted she come home to help. This remained a sore point. Mom often said she could not have been a nurse. She never returned to New York, though she'd sing "East Side, West Side" and talk about the thrill of walking into the library at Columbia, and the professor who'd urged her to pursue doctoral studies.

Her father had been a rural veterinarian and gold medalist from the University of Toronto who'd accepted a university professorship just before he died. She was three. Her mother remarried and would not discuss her first husband.

I'd quiz Mom about this. She'd say: "If I'd gone on studying, I wouldn't have had you, so things worked out for the best." Then she'd add: "Every time you do what's right, even if you feel it requires a sacrifice, life will surprise you with its blessings."

When I won the book prize for grade nine, Mom told me she thought I would like university, but that whatever money they could save for higher education would go to support my brother who would become the bread-winner for a family. She suggested that, if I worked hard, I might earn a scholarship.

When it was time to do a job study in grade ten, I said I wanted to be an anthropologist. Mom drove me out to UBC to interview a professor in the basement of the library. He told me I should count on another twelve years of study after I finished high school. Twelve years! When I asked him where anthropologists worked, he waved his arm around at some dusty artifacts and shelves of books. "Oh, in places like this." On the drive home Mom recommended one year of teacher training, in case something happened to my husband.

Mom loved, and always praised, the handsome man she'd married, and she prized the family that arose from their complex, contradictory, creative lives. She also loved her work, and did it with confidence, imagination, insight, and considerable success.

And yet, some part of her felt she hadn't been a "proper" wife and mother. I knew she wanted to redeem this "failure" by producing a conventional daughter, and that this was to be my job.

I did my best. To her great satisfaction, I married young and produced three grandchildren while still in my twenties. My husband was a good provider and a good person but he believed in a patriarchal family. He insisted—when I talked about wanting my own career—that I had a full-time job at home. I kept on studying, paying for university courses out of my Family Allowance cheques, and slowly completed two masters degrees. When one of my professors urged me to go on and do a PhD, my husband said one doctorate (his) was enough in a family.

We've all come a long way since then. I did eventually leave that marriage, work outside the home, complete a doctorate and pursue a career (in education!).

One of the deepest patterns in my life—insecurity about my vocation, guilt around fulfilling it, guilt around not fulfilling it—is an echo from my mother. Who would she have been if she'd been able to set anxiety about "real motherhood" aside? Who would I have been if she'd been able to do this?

Who's Sorry Now?

Jeanette Lynes

Connie Francis wants to know, belts the question
while my mother hoists metal bowls
under udders, switches on thumping vacuums
that yank the milk into a big tank. Apparently I was
there, tucked in my stroller, watching her chore
while the transistor, with its film of barn-dust
chittered on and I jiggled to Connie, Paul Anka,
The Everly Brothers crooning through the dust.
She said I could pick up any tune *just like that.*
I'm glad I had a talent.
The cows plodded in on their large, terrible hooves,
their teats morose, blotchy, veined, set to explode.
I can still pluck a song
from clouded air, can picture those teats,
the ugliest sight in the world—if you'd seen them
you'd have lived your life like mine, fleeing dairy.

THE GIFT

Ruth Roach Pierson

1.
Brought up on the idea it's better to give, the young girl has given
her mother a gift she openly scorns as ugly, cheap: a sewing kit
the girl loved for its cylindrical shape like a box for a very tall hat.
Its material—cardboard encased in quilted turquoise plastic
with a handle of gold braided cord and a shelf inside
that lifted out, a round, shallow tray divided
into wedge-shaped pieces like a pie.

Forty years later the daughter has returned to sort through
her mother's cupboards, drawers, and closets full of dresses,
shoes, coats, shelves piled with sweaters, hats and yards of fabric
already chalk marked and cut along the lines of tissue-paper
patterns pinned to the cloth. And there, in a corner: the sewing
kit crammed with thread-wound bobbins and spools, mending
yarn, buttons, needles, pins, and pinking shears—a crack
in the turquoise plastic, the gold braid of the handle frayed.

2.
My always impeccably-groomed mother
sits bare-assed,
tied to a potty chair on wheels,
scant apron across her lap:
private parts
no longer private here.
Age has strip-mined her mind,
stretched the skin on her head skull-tight,
shrivelled her body so thin the wedding ring
she wore for more than fifty years
slipped off her finger.

Front tooth chipped,
she gives me a hag's leer,
grabs my hand, begs
take me out of this place
anywhere

home. But home has suffered a diaspora:
the objects that defined her life
dispersed to nephew, niece, neighbour—
muffin tins, piano, embroidered
pillow cases—
a household hit by hurricane.
I spoon ice cream
between her gums;
she confides in me,
a stranger, how hard
it is to mother a daughter
who expects too much,
demands that she be perfect. Leaning in I whisper
But you were:

it was so easy
to leave in your hands the iron
you snatched from mine,
to leave to you the needles and pins,
scrub mop, the crack in the lid
of the flowered tea pot.

3.
I know, when she visits at night, who she is. Take last night:
swigging champagne, knocking it back straight out of the bottle
as she slammed down winning hands and laughed it up with
Auntie Viv and Cousin Chris under the slanted ceiling of my
teenage bedroom. I stood off in a corner pulling piles of folded
cloths from a closet, holding myself back, thinking—
how strange to see my teetotal mother let go.

She always ran a tight ship, pitching housework goals so high
I failed to learn to cook or can; my only task, besides the dinner
dishes, to hang out the wash: she trusted me with that; and how
I loved to hold up each dripping piece, press the notch
of the wooden peg down tight over the line, and in twilight
gather the sheets, pants, shirts, towels, now dry,
and cart them in, blended with the scent of grass.

We never shared a drink, or a laugh, that I remember.
Clothes were our bond, even though she thought I ironed wrinkles
in instead of out and never taught me how to sew. Shopping: we
met on common ground. Sporting hats, gloves, heels, we'd go
downtown, to Frederic's or the Bon, visit the tea room, take a look
around—she'd lean back in the fitting room chair, sizing up the
skirt and sweater I try on.

My Life Is Not My Own

Carla Hartsfield

There's nothing like sitting up high in the mimosa tree on a warm April day. They're easy to climb, even in your checkerboard smock dress with the red ribbon sash. Your boxy black leather-and-suede shoes with candy cane laces are the only deterrent. The shoes have slick soles and make climbing the tree precarious. You hate your corrective shoes and the twice-yearly visit to the podiatrist. You won't own a pair of real tennis shoes until you try out for drill team in grade eight. Your feet are flat as pancakes, just like your dad's. Worse, you were born with your hip joints facing inward. One night at age two, you try crawling to the bathroom, a steel rod harnessed between your feet. You'll stop wearing the brace after one year, as it fails to give you turn out; ballet lessons will never be an option.

But, you're far away from that memory, laughing high up in the mimosa. Your mother thinks you're on the Mark Twain schoolyard, playing a game of touch football with the minister's son, Robby. There would be other kids from your class: best friend, Cheryl, and Hal. Hal nurses a crush on you until you're both in your mid-twenties, but that knowledge is not accessible yet, nor relevant.

You smile, not because you've hidden yourself away, and the Texas air is so joyous and pleasant, but because you've written your first story. It's about Robby, and the tremendous crush you've got on this dark-haired hunk. You're only ten but quite tall, willowy, mature. Everyone says so. Your mother took you bra shopping the other day, and you love the white stretch cotton and elastic cups encasing your budding breasts. Your story is about kissing

Robby, the events and conversation leading up to that moment. It's nighttime when it happens, a sultry August evening and bright crescent moon inserted between the branches of this very tree. Fireflies flicker about your heads as you lean toward each other, lips softly touching before the full kiss takes hold.

∽

"Carla Jean!" my mother screams. I assume she's standing on our concrete porch. I hear the gate to our chain-link fence creak open, slam shut. I can't see her yet, don't want to. I can already tell she's fuming. What did I do this time? It was always something, an endless train of transgressions.

I sense she's under the mimosa now, my safety zone, her Mom Radar parked in overdrive. "You better get down out of that tree, Miss Priss, and explain yourself." She's waving two sheets of binder paper. *Oh no: my story.* I had folded it into thirds and fourths and sixths, so small it became this insignificant triangle of paper deep in the recesses of my red-plaid school bag. Or so I thought.

"I mean it, Carla Jean," she huffs, her voice an ear-piercing twang. "I'm gonna get my belt. You'll wish you'd never been born after I tan your hide."

I already wished I'd never been born, as long ago as that nighttime trawl to the bathroom, my feet imprisoned. Early on I sensed a need to hide, remain silent at all costs. Now this. How my mother screams in a Methodist minister's yard! The parsonage is directly behind our house across the alley. But, since she believes Methodists are going to hell along with the other heathens and Christians not believing in her version of the Bible, and because her personal Jesus has made her sinless, it's perfectly fine to yell at me underneath the mimosa in the minister's yard.

Resigned, fatalistic as only a child can be, I flip onto my stomach and start sliding down. My mother wears a cotton sack dress, some godawful garish print with zipper up the front, her face puffy and red. I anchor one slippery, boxy shoe, then jump easily onto the grass. I'm in for it, and yet, even then, I believed my imagination was a good thing, my saving grace.

∽

In 1948, my parents were wed at the local preacher's house, my mother's sister, Martha Jean, and husband, Doolin, the only attendees. My mother wore a royal blue skirt and long-sleeved white silk blouse with gold buttons. She didn't wear a hat or veil, unusual at the time, and there are no pictures, maybe more unusual. The newlyweds were only nineteen and fourteen, teenagers playing dress-up. My mother could pass for twenty-five, though, a cross between Elizabeth Taylor and Jane Russell. Her breasts, like those of that Hollywood star Howard Hughes made famous, were legend and, my father's obsession, proven by the number of cashmere sweater sets he bought her. My mother liked to wear bright red lipstick with no other makeup, her lustrous black hair, naturally curly and parted on the side. Every photo from this era shows a beautiful young woman in Texas-style haute couture standing in a cotton field. These creations came courtesy of my grandmother, Carrie, a meticulous and talented seamstress. Carrie could sew anything, even the cloud-like strapless ball gown for her youngest daughter's high school prom. My mother was crowned duchess that night—a knock-out, no question—and even weirder, already a married woman.

The trouble was, my father fell in love, but I suspect he mainly fell for a body and face. I also suspect my mother was like any other teenager. She wanted to date a variety of boys, vamp and tease, but that was pretty much it. This was the beginning of the baby boom and post-war prosperity, suburban track housing and no petting below the waist, a border crossing into the conformist 1950s. In rural Texas if you wanted to have sex you got married.

Except, my mother didn't want to have sex. Later, she would brag to me how she put my father off during their honeymoon. This is how I remember their fifty-one-year marriage: my father's silent, angry frustration, my mother's taunting attitude, her physical as well as emotional brain washing. *What? I didn't hit you, Carla. You've imagined that. No Gene, we can't have sex. Not unless you buy me a new dress or diamond or Cadillac.* Because my father was adopted into a wealthy family, money wasn't an issue, initially, even though he did his best to spend his inheritance before I reached adulthood. So by the time my sister and I began university, there wasn't much left. His own mother had given him up at three months because of an affair. But, it was 1930, the start of the Great Depression. So my father, technically, was illegitimate. Karmic or Freudian, I sometimes wondered if my mother was just a substitute for the mother he never knew.

∽

My mother once admitted she didn't know females could have orgasms until after I was born. She would have been in her early thirties, well, about the time she found my story. Her family doctor, as part of a routine physical, asked if she was happy with her sex life. He also used the "O" word. I'm certain Dr. Russell didn't know she married way too young. "Mary," he said, in his friendly doctor voice, "why don't you have a talk with that nice husband of yours? Read this in bed together." He then handed over a pamphlet on oral sex, masturbation and the like.

I suppose my mother read it, though I'm fairly certain she never showed it to my father. One day, while giving me a Toni home permanent, she blurted out: "Men just wanna see your whoopie cakes jiggle. Keep 'em out of your pants, Carla Jean. Better to have em' knockin' on the door than inside the gate."

Huh? At ten, I could barely imagine kissing and only the most chaste sort of cinematic one. What would letting a boy in my pants entail? Naturally, I felt fear. And excitement. What could be so bad, really? That's the kind of kid I was, curiouser and curiouser. Alice had nothing on me.

But, from the day of the Mimosa Tree Incident, my life was not my own, especially what I wrote. My mother broke into my room, cracked open my diaries, somehow finding the miniature keys hidden beneath my mattress or inside a pillow case. It didn't matter where I hid them. So I stopped telling the truth. I wrote what I thought she wanted to read. It worked, but only for a short time.

∽

It's the summer of 1976. I've begun my first serious affair with a fellow pianist and composition major at the University of Texas. Perry and I became friends after meeting at freshman orientation, when he heard me playing Beethoven's famous *Sonata Pathetique*. Two years seemed like a reasonable time to date before having sex. It was the mid-seventies; I considered myself a prude of the first order because, at nineteen, I was the only virgin I knew.

When Perry arrives at my house for the Fourth of July holiday, we've only done it a couple of times. I'm not aware that he's stored condoms in his suitcase. While we're out one afternoon, my mother methodically searches his bag, finding what she's looking for. Upon our return, she demands Perry leave the house without telling him why. He complies, shaking his head and more than angry. When I hear the engine start on his car, I have this urge to fly out of the house and jump in with him, never to return. When it comes to dealing with my mother, there were too many times when I should have listened to that still, small voice within, though didn't.

I watch Perry drive off, feeling panic. When I turn around my mother is standing by the fireplace, her dark eyes shifting rapidly. She announces Perry and I will wed in the fall. Her tone is matter-of-fact, calculated. There is no discussion about how I feel.

My father is present but silent for this interview. If I refuse to marry I will get a job, live at home, not be allowed to date or pursue a university education. Since I've just been accepted to study piano with John Perry, *the* top piano teacher in North America, I open my mouth as if to reply, then close it quickly. In future, more craziness is due to top this craziness. Because of my youth and fear of the woman who claims she is my biological mother, I suspect once again, my life is not my own.

∽

Love is a strange device. I use the word device on purpose. To my mother, love meant unquestioning obedience. Her God was the angry sort, an Old Testament relic who rebuked and penalized. My mother *thinks* she loves me, but like her views on religion, it's her own special brand. I was never held, stroked or kissed as a child. She blamed Doctor Spock, that 50s authority on diapering and kid rebellion. So I grew up with an untreatable hybrid of A.D.D.: Affection Deficit Disorder.

Only in mid-life do you figure out what happened. Your mother was attempting to find common ground between you. As you had no other commonality, she tried marrying you off against your will. Her own choices around marriage and sexual freedom had been truncated, in effect, capping her emotional development—so why not put on a stopper on yours? Even when you attempted to change the story in your diaries and heart only to please her, divorce court won out.

For more than half your life, your authentic voice goes underground. That self takes her poems and stories and sexual experiences to a place nobody can reach. After years of psychotherapy you recover lost memory, feel safe enough to allow that girl high up in the mimosa tree to bloom, feet swinging. But, you would have to untie the cast-iron apron strings, immigrate to Canada, and jump headlong into an isolated world with no safety net, to realize it.

MOVING

Elizabeth Greene

At seven, I hated to leave that house behind,
the Rose of Sharon tree outside my window,
the blueberry bushes, sandbox, swings.

        To leave the ghosts
of my first cats—Smokey I, Smokey II,
Gray Greene, Copper and Felina. Five cats
in five years, vanished. My mother
too afraid of death to bury or mourn them.

        Hated to leave my friends,
double-jointed Linda who could walk
on her hands; Valerie, who ate fish on Friday.

        Didn't understand that
for my mother age seven meant tragedy,
the age her little brother was hit by a car
nearly thirty years before, didn't understand
she might have felt disaster hovering:

        time to move. Closing day
came in the midst of storms. *Never put off a closing,*
our lawyer said. The sale closed. The next day,
the roof blew off.

In our new house, the power failed,
we weren't sure about the furnace.
and we stayed with a friend for a month.
At seven, I felt the best of my life was over.

THE TORY CANDIDATE COMES TO CALL

Alice Major

in her well-cut tweeds, a knock at the door
of the flat where the bairns are colouring
on the carpet in front of the fire,
and the pots are preparing to boil.

Mary answers the knock,
and she's a fragment of cordite
under the rap of a hammer,
when the candidate, polite

and bloody condescending,
asks for her vote, *Mrs. Major,* to get
those Labour MPs out of parliament.
They'll ruin the country.

The Red Clyde boils in Mary's veins.
You with your handbag and pearls.
You'd ruin the workers.
Her girls, her seed pearls, look up.

She's not about to give back
the small new monthly cheque,
the family allowance, that lets her buy
her daughters their good oxfords.

The would-be member of parliament
is sent with a flea in her ear
back down the tenement's stone stairs
like a ladder down silk stockings.

MY MOTHER TAUGHT ME

Zöe Landale

Be careful what you wish for, you just might get it.

What the Fifties brought my mother were the things she'd always wanted: marriage to an educated, professional man and four children. My mother was one of those women who really wanted kids, had thought about having babies since she was sixteen. She got to live out her dream, though in my mind, it was more like a prolonged nightmare. *Housewife* has become such a pejorative word, it's important to remember how much actual physical labour these women accomplished, and how responsible they themselves felt their way of life was.

Talk about keeping the home fires burning: that comes from the literal, the stoking of wood and coal furnaces. During an Ottawa winter, my mother was down in the basement every couple of hours, shoveling in the fuel which kept the cat's milk on the kitchen floor from freezing.

Life must go forward clean.

The first thing I learned, I learned from my mother, was that in any household crisis—and there were many—it was essential the life of the family go forward clean. One of my earliest memories is the wringer washer we had in the basement. While an improvement over a scrub board and kettles of boiling water, the previous method, it took considerable effort to wash a family's load of dirty laundry, put it through the wringer, then back in to agitate, rinse, wring, and then finally, hang out on the line with clothespins to dry. In Ottawa, depending on the time of year, the laundry would freeze stiff on the line.

"When I was living in India with my kids," a friend told me recently, "it took half a day to do our laundry. I have a picture of the goddess Lakshmi by my washing machine now and each time I do a load, I say *thank you.*" My mother would've been able to relate to that.

At home, we also dusted and polished furniture, vacuumed, washed and waxed the kitchen floor. Mum was especially tough on dirty floors. It was a good day for our family when products like Mop n' Glow were invented. I remember being so pleased not to have to go down on hands and knees to put paste wax on anymore while Mum followed behind, polishing the floor with the buffer, a heavy square thing like a mop with weights.

When I remember the kitchen of the house in Vancouver we moved to when I was nine, there's always the tang of lemon floor cleaner, the ancient linoleum metamorphosed to a satiny glow with the magic of the Mop n' Glow that Mum poured into a bucket of water. The smell was intensely comforting. When the rest of the world whirled as if it would throw me off, I could rest upon that cleanliness.

There's no shame in hard work.

My father once told me: "I have never, ever in my life, seen a woman work the way your mother works."

When my parents split up, for us kids it was a relief in a way, as the fights between Mum and Dad had been just awful. Only three other kids that I knew of in my school of twelve hundred had divorced parents. My dad, who struggled with alcohol and a breakdown, paid zero child support; ergo Mum had to get a paying job and that rather quickly. ("Always make sure you have your own money," she often told my sister and me in later years. She obviously felt her lack of money during the marriage and divorce was her fault instead of seeing it as simply as the partner with no money has no power, either.)

My mother, who had an Honour's degree in English and History from the University of Toronto, was overeducated for something like selling shoes and under qualified for anything that paid well or was half-way interesting. For a few months she drove a school bus, but she couldn't get in enough hours to feed a family. So she started work at Maclure's Taxi. They were the only place who'd hire longhairs, immigrants and women as drivers. Other companies looked down their noses at Maclure's. As befitted their status, Maclure's territory was the East End.

Gratitude.

Mum, who was West Side to the roots of her dark dyed hair, never complained about her transition from housewife to taxi driver. She went from being wife of the director of the Vancouver Art Gallery to a nobody. As I was the eldest child, and confidante, she did tell me how hurt she was that none of the society families with whom she'd been socializing a few times a month kept in touch with her. But mainly she emphasized how much she was learning. When she got home, she'd tell us stories about her work day. Listening to her, the city of Vancouver became a different place. I saw the waterfront in its true importance, Vancouver as an international port. Sailors loomed largely in her stories. Discreetly—I understood but the younger kids didn't—Mum said there were Certain Destinations that sailors always wanted. Certain houses. And her tips went up when she found out where they were.

Mum tried to get me to help with the endless flowerbeds that came with our house, but one plant looked the same as another to me and I did a lot of damage before I was permanently removed from garden duties. We kids got to pick which room in the house we'd clean thoroughly once a week.

After a year of driving, Mum went back to university. She got her teaching degree and then a job teaching high school. Sometimes she'd teach all day, come home, put her feet up for twenty minutes, get us all something to eat, and go out and teach night school. I was the eldest and I helped as best I could. At fourteen, I learned to cook, plan menus, go grocery shopping.

But through this turmoil our house was clean, and even the youngest child learned to operate the washing machine.

Retail therapy.

When I was a teenager and feeling especially desolate about something, Mum would say: "Let's go shopping." I might mutter something graceless from the chair in which I was huddled, but secretly, I would start to feel better right away. Mum's store of choice was almost invariably Woodward's, in those days a department store of two floors that seemed vast at the time, and laughably tiny in retrospect. Inside, a fluorescent-lit calm prevailed. Escalators circulated serenely on their endless loop, elevator Muzak prevailed, and clerks were found in profusion, not just behind the cash desks, but in between, available to help shoppers. This is something only the most expensive retail outlets have now, but at the time, it was the norm, and we always made liberal use of the clerks' help in finding navy blue shorts for gym, or a skirt small enough for a skinny girl with no hips.

After our purchases had been made, we'd have lunch out. This was a Big Deal. While we talked about the different places we might go, there really wasn't any doubt. We'd go to the windowless restaurant in Woodward's basement, with its decor of cosy browns. What we ordered was always the same: shrimp sandwiches on toasted cheese bread, with chocolate milkshakes. I was always guiltily conscious of how much that lunch was costing us.

Part of the joy of the meal out was discussing what Mum had bought for me and deciding yes, it was a real bargain, or it suited me marvellously, in short that we had made the right choice. We'd go home with a glow on. "It's power," Mum said. "Spending money is power." It always worked. I cheered right up.

The importance of family.

Mum's most important teaching, though, one she lived her life by, was the importance of family. Friends were wonderful—two in other cities were lifelong—but friends moved. Even if I'd been close with someone, when she moved, we would grow apart. I had to lose quite a number of friends before I came close to Mum's view. In her book, friends were dessert, so to speak, while family was meat and potatoes. We took Mum for granted then. It took me another thirty years to understand she was our family's central strength, our anchor. After she passed on, our family felt like we'd all been blown to opposite ends of the galaxy. It took us sibs three years to put Mum's teachings into practice and re-establish our bonds.

Women are sugar and spice and iron.

Without the Fifties and the too-tight-shoe marriage, Mum wouldn't have had her dream of kids and staying home to look after us. But as the anxious oldest child, I still see her, two brown paper bags of groceries, one in each arm, and a toddler clinging to her leg, getting out of the family's robin's egg blue station wagon. She'd climb the back stairs, put the groceries away, and then, oh joy, it was time for dinner and she was the one making it. Afterwards we kids would do dishes, and Mum might do ironing (every fabric then wrinkled horribly) or, in later years, do marking. It was the sheer endless household labour that I remember my mother doing, that and her terror if she didn't make enough money, The Authorities—she referred to them in caps—would take us, her kids, from her.

It never happened, of course. It was a dark bat-fear with little foundation in reality. Somehow, Mum paid the bills. Maybe my beef isn't so much with the Fifties holding my mother in a straitjacket as the very mention of that time makes me feel shame and a nagging dread. The bank manager laughed in her face when she asked for a loan to tide us over the summer the first year she taught. Mom went out and got a minimum wage job working for the Parks and Recreation. My dad did sign over the house to her. That brought a new set of problems. "The bank manager wanted your father to cosign for the mortgage, or my father" (thirty years dead), Mum said bitterly. "A male, any male, would do."

I understood her outrage; I shared it. I was intensely aware of what my mother suffered and also, too, of what she achieved: we always had a clean cloth on the table and food to put on it. Professionally too, she succeeded. Each year she'd come home with half a dozen cards from students saying how she'd changed their lives. I honour my mother—she was a valiant woman, a fighter, a sparrow who finagled her way around the bank manager who'd patronized her. She never missed a payment on the mortgage, either, though fear about the recurring possibility was thick as smoke over Mordor. In retrospect, I wish she'd had friends who lived close, a support network. But maybe she didn't have time for anything but family and work.

Mum always made time to take us four kids to the library and talk about books; we'd come home each week with a waist-high wicker laundry hamper quite full. It took one person on either side to carry the thing. At home, we had a massive two volume OED handy to the supper table to settle disputes about the meaning or pronunciation of words. Mum often jumped up from a meal to consult the relevant volume. I am proud to say she also drove with a dictionary in her glove compartment.

OVERCOATS: HERS AND HERS

Susan Helwig

My mother
a stone
who wanted me for a mountain

We sit in overcoats
she asks how I feel about her dying
nothing is what I feel
but where to hide?

First I blame her coat
she must take it off
set an example
show me what's inside

When she doesn't budge
I get up and set our table
with platitudes, knives

"I can't believe ..."
"Remember the time ..."
"You know, Dad never really ..."

Ah, *mon petit chou!*
You hoped to grow an elm when you had me
but too soon used, too much bent
down from heights that we forgot
we both were reaching for.

MAKE IT GLOW

Penn Kemp

For those mothers who remain
ashore and shoring, mending
holes, cutting cords,
gathering stray strands:

Weave the common thread
wide and strong. Make it hold.

Make it glow like that
first cord we almost
remember, the one
cut off too soon.

NOT DICK AND JANE

Family Herald and Weekly Star, October 4, 1951

AMATEUR IN THE HOUSE

*Is there any way a loving husband can tell his loving wife
that as a nightingale she is a sparrow, and still not
ruffle her feathers?*

By WILLIAM SAMBROT

My Mother, My 1950s

Sharon Thesen

I was walking home along Tranquille Road with a pack of Black Cats. It was 1955 or '56, I was nine or ten years old, I was wearing a pair of shorts but that's all—no shirt, no shoes. Tranquille Road was the main highway from North Kamloops that led to the green, restful grandeur of Tranquille Sanitorium, where my mother had, fairly recently, spent two years recovering from tuberculosis. The cars and trucks sped by in both directions. My mother had given me the quarter to buy the cigarettes with, but hadn't seen to it that I was dressed properly. I suddenly felt ashamed, and hurried back home.

My father worked for low wages in the office at the Royalite oil refinery. Fathers would come home from work and watch you do the cartwheel you'd been practising, or have a look at the flat tire on your bike. In the stifling house, we'd eat supper, then go back outside until it cooled down enough to go to bed. I hardly remember winters. It was always hot out. The nearby North Thompson River would do for cooling off—in places there was a bit of a beach, or a sandbar you could get to. The powerful current pulled your body insistently in one direction. You could swim like a champion downstream, but would have to fight to get back to shore; and then you'd scramble in your wet bathing suit through pungent willow bushes to where families like ours laid out potato salad and hot dogs and yelled at their kids.

Those suppers by the river would be on weeknights, after work. Payday was every other Friday, and my parents would buy a case of beer and invite their friends over to the house. My mother was happy to be out of "the San" and living with her popular, good-looking, musical husband again. In the small crimp-edge photos of that time, she looks like Elizabeth Taylor—the curviness in a light-coloured shirtwaist dress, the short dark hairstyle. My father wore a blond crew cut, a white T-shirt, a smile. I would lie awake during their parties listening to the lyrics of "The Shady Lady from Shady Lane" and "I Want to Live in a Little Grass Shack" and the punchlines of dirty jokes. It was seldom that I heard my mother's peals of laughter, her happiness and pleasure. Mom was often in a bad mood: angry pork chops, angry rug flapping, angry laundry on the line. We stayed out of her way. We were giving her a Nervous Breakdown; she'd have to go to *Crease Clinic*, down at the coast. The unhappy mothers whose children drove them Totally Insane were sent to *Riverview*, and those mothers never came back. So we had to be good. After living in several different but equally inadequate houses in an area of orchards and small farms outside of North Kamloops called Brocklehurst (now chock-a-block with subdivisions, malls, schools, arenas, and churches), we moved to Prince George in the middle of the winter in which 1959 turned into 1960.

The half decade 1955-60 were my years of independent childhood, the years that, some say, form your essential outlook. It was not the "white picket fence" sheltered, middle class world portrayed in contemporary (and condescending) images of the time. My younger brother and I roamed the cougar-infested gullies and pine gulches, took fruit from nearby orchards, checked each other's heads and ears for ticks. We suffered the humiliating illnesses of the poor. But for me, those years, that perpetual summer, was marked most of all by physical and imaginative freedom, and, when I think of it now, an astonishing degree of inventiveness, daring, and self-reliance. Plus, there was a certain sense that things could get better. As my father gained promotions at Royalite, so my parents began to aspire to a more middle-class existence. My mother was still processing her own garden produce on a wood stove and we children slept three to a room, but things were looking up. A TV set, for example. We held our breath as it was plugged in and switched on, but the CBC Indian chief logo would be the only thing on the screen until 3 in the afternoon. I loved going to school, where I was a favourite of my teacher, Mrs. Coulpier. My new little sister was adorable. Soon I was twelve and had a mad crush on Elvis Presley.

These were the 1950s I knew. My mother's experience of that time must have included exhaustion, boredom, and frustration. She had only recently been discharged from Tranquille, and the contrast between the enforced days and months of bed rest and the physical demands of being home with two, and then three, small children must have been overwhelming. She was not maternal by nature and told me some time ago that, in those days, women had babies only because "that's just what everybody did." As a young girl, she had loved going to school and has often said how much she would have enjoyed going to university. But she was called home halfway through grade ten to look after her younger half-siblings when her own mother became ill with cancer. Her marriage to my father at nineteen was a socially-approved escape from that life. I was born the following year, in 1946. Had my mother been born twenty years later, she might have had a more fulfilling, perhaps a much easier, life. But life is never easy, despite appearances, and we are indelibly pressed and formed by our times and places. The string-saving haggard grandmothers who "went through" the Great Depression are now the Botoxed Lululemon-wearing grandmothers going through their own depressions. The mothers of the Fifties—the ones of my family's class—worked to keep things together without any of the social, financial, or therapeutic support now taken for granted. They were young—marriage and children by age twenty-two was common—and they were probably stunned by the responsibilities they suddenly faced. They really did do their best, even if they didn't sometimes, or couldn't.

The Fifties era we are admonished about today (and which it would be silly to merely idealize) evokes a lurid tableau: spanked children; repression and authoritarian control via church and school; sexism, racism, and homophobia; compulsory heterosexuality; profound family dysfunction behind the "white picket fence" of conformity, men in grey flannel suits and women servile and housebound—in short, every sin known to postmodernism, feminism, atheism, multiculturalism, and political correctness. The Fifties were indeed a time when institutions conspired to ensure white, male hegemony in every area of life. It's the era most easily mocked (because of the risible transparency of its propagandas), the one compared to which the obvious merits of our own enlightened time shine most brightly. The evil lurking behind the "white picket fence" remains a sturdy trope even today. The gaiety of *Ozzie and Harriet* and the patriarchal values of *Leave It To Beaver* are stock items in the list of offensive and/or ridiculous Fifties icons—and add to that atrocious racism and the Cold War. It is true that many people suffered horribly in the Fifties because of prejudice, ignorance, and fear. These sufferings continue to be documented, and some of their institutional perpetrators prosecuted in the courts. But I am not so sure that suffering hasn't shape-shifted into numerous and insidious forms in our own day, forms that may in later decades be seen as destructive as those endured by many groups and individuals then.

Canada in the 1950s was, I think, a much different country from the United States, but similar in its general trajectory, with glimmerings of change (both threatening and exhilarating) and prosperity (always exhilarating) on the horizon. The full force of that change would be in the Sixties, but the vanguard of the Sixties were the writers, painters, architects, film-makers, civil rights workers, and musicians of the Fifties. Their now-classic art forms and social reforms still define what is modern, admirable, and cool. Disapproving accounts of beatnik antics published in *Life* magazine in the late '50s were thrilling to me; I aspired to such a life and later tried to approximate its trappings—burlap curtains, Eric Dolphy records, black berets, foreign movies. Times were changing. California-style youth culture would soon become the pre-eminent expression of the only value we now take seriously: lifestyle choices. A white picket fence was beyond my mother's wildest dreams, and mine as well. She may have sent me out half-dressed to buy cigarettes, but her smokes were breaks in a back-breaking day; and anyway at age nine or ten I looked a couple of years younger. Then, "everybody" smoked, and "everybody" had two kids and another on the way. And no woman was ever "pregnant": she was "expecting," and she wouldn't have turned down a cold beer on a hot afternoon, while the older kids were out on their bikes on the gravel roads that led to the river.

LET US ANSWER TO OUR NAMES

Marilynn Rudi

Christened Mary Dolena
mother grew up Doll or Dolly
at the long kitchen table,
turnip fields and gravel roads,
her name a dirty dishrag
she wished to wring clean.

When the war began
she became Mary,
dressed in her RCAF suit
tinkling good sense and virtue
like silver bells.

Father's papers destroyed
by himself or war
he came to Canada Osvald
quickly changed to Oswald.

"Call me Ozzie," he urged new friends,
like Ozzie and Harriet on TV.
He slid her to the passenger side
of her Studebaker and drove.
"Call me Ozzie," and she did
for fifty years.

He called her *you* or
                          nothing at all.

His last wintry month
curled on chesterfield
legs useless, core eaten
demanding food water morphine.

"He's started calling me by name," she told me.
"He *has* to."

It was true—
I heard him cry past midnight
tongue struggling with the sounds.
Somewhat deaf
she's sleeping soundly at eighty-two
not hearing a word.

The House with Many Doors

Marjorie Simmins

People are always leaving. There are many doors inside our house and three doors leading out of our house. People move from room to room, upstairs and down, then to the basement rooms, slamming doors behind them. There are bells tied to the curtain rod on the back door. The bells jangle when the door is slammed shut. The front door is heavy. My brother uses it the most. My Mum and sisters don't slam that one. They prefer the lighter doors. You don't have to be angry to slam a door. You might just want to be heard for some reason. Everyone in the house slams doors. Or just shuts them hard. It's how we talk right now.

I step through one of the five doorways leading into the kitchen. The room is empty and cold.

I could go back upstairs, get a sweater. But I don't want to wake Mum. Sometimes she has a mid-afternoon nap on Saturdays. Once she was sleeping so hard I couldn't even shake her awake. That scared me. No more Valium, she says now. Now she wakes easily again. I stood in the doorway of her room before I came back downstairs. Face to the wall, she had turned over, said, "Hello, little love," then rolled back to the wall again.

She looks funny in that small bed in my brother's old room.

Which reminds me.

I slip through two doors into my parents' old bedroom. The double bed is made up tidily and there are books in the shelf of the headboard. The books are boring. I've checked them many times. But there are things on the bureau that interest me. 711 Eau de Parfum. A paisley ascot. One cuff-link. Parent stuff. Beyond these, a bottle I can just reach.

Aqua-Velva aftershave. The turquoise liquid makes the centre of me go soft with colour-happiness. Could be mermaid water. The bottle is almost full. He will return for it. And for us, of course.

My red-haired sister, five years older than me, scorns me for this idea. "You really think he's coming back, don't you?" she asked last week, when she caught me smelling the aftershave. She shook her head: "Stupid." She melted away.

My red-haired sister can appear out of nowhere; she doesn't even need doors. She has a hunger to hurt, like a nasty cat with sharp claws. She scratches Mum, mostly. Mum pretends it doesn't hurt. We all look away, because it hurts everyone, but we don't know what to do. Fourteen years old and she frightens all of us. That's the reason the mermaid water helps. Just for a moment of softness inside. I think my red-haired sister misses Dad, even though she says she hates him. It feels like she hates all of us.

She is staying at a friend's house this weekend. I am glad.

My blonde-haired sister, seven years older than me, isn't here very much these days. Dad left last year, when the snowdrops came up in the garden. My blonde-haired sister's face is like a whole garden of flowers, since she met her boyfriend, also last year. But she is furious at Dad too.

I think I'll watch some TV. "Idiot box," my parents call it. But Mum enjoys it more than Dad ever did. On Friday nights we all watch TV together. We have "Friday night treats," a phrase Mum made up. TGIF, she says on a Friday night. We pass around bowls of Jujubes and Bridge Mix and pieces of Burnt Almond chocolate bars. We aren't allowed Coke during the week, but we drink it on Friday night. Everyone seems lighter, happier on a Friday night.

I look up from *Captain Kangaroo* to see my mother.

"Hungry?" she asks. I had Tang and toast, and tell her this. I even remembered to put the glass and plate in the sink, and didn't leave it here on the table in front of me in the family room. She hates it when we eat in here, and make a mess. My brother is 12 and I am 9; we don't do much housework. Mum used to do it throughout the day, along with the ironing, grocery shopping and meal making. Now she drives a cab and can't keep up with the housework or the gardening. This distresses her. She loves order and a well-run house.

"We had maids growing up," she says sometimes. My sisters, brother and I find it hard to picture this. Maids are for rich people. Not for people with second mortgages and cars that need repair. We had a home in London, Ontario and a cottage on the lake, in Bayfield, she explains, eyes distant with happy memories. Why I didn't even know how to cook, she'd tell us with pride, until after the Air Force, when I went to university. Her roommates teased her into the kitchen, she said.

My father's new girlfriend—"Daddy's *whore*," says my red-haired sister—is a very good cook, our father tells us. This knowledge hurts me.

It is too quiet in the kitchen. I look over my shoulder from my spot on the couch. Mum is standing in the centre of the room. Her shoulders are rising up and down. It looks like she is laughing.

Sadness and anger. With Mum, it's hard to pry those two feelings apart. Sometimes I think she's just sad and then I see the shimmer of rage in her eyes. Mostly I see fatigue. I feel bad. Our lives feel so heavy sometimes. I can't find the right things to do, to make Mum feel better.

I stand in the doorway. Everything is still around us, except for a boiling kettle on the stove. Mum hasn't had her tea yet. This hurts me too. Too much sadness, even before her first cup of sugared, black tea. Of the five purple doors, four are closed. All that dark colour set against white. Somehow it seems like the room is pushing in. It's hard to breathe in this cold place.

"I am going to pack us a bag," she says. "We are going away."

Now I really can't breathe. My brother. He's downstairs sleeping. If he wakes up and we are gone, maybe he'll go too. He isn't mean like my red-haired sister and he's here most of the time. We laugh together, listen to records. He's teaching me how to play poker. I can't lose him too.

"I'll write a note for your brother. He'll be fine for a day."

I open my mouth and a spiral of distress comes out. A cat, her tail stepped on.

"Stop it. It's only today and part of tomorrow." She is moving briskly now, talking to herself. "Write a note, put it by his place at the table; don't forget a book, need a book, sweaters too ..."

Vancouver is a pearl today. From a cold kitchen we step out to a mild, blossom-scented world. The clouds are gold-rimmed and tumbling on a northwest wind, the sky behind a light-shot blue. The navy blue ocean has curled white tips on it, like the boiled icing you put on an angel food cake. We drive alongside English Bay. Saturday morning and the downtown streets are busy. Sailboats skim by the Planetarium. Farther out in the harbour there are orange-bottomed freighters. Yellow and red popcorn stands are set one block apart all along Pacific Avenue. My breakfast has worn off and the scent of buttery popped corn makes my stomach grumble. I wonder when we'll stop, where we are going to spend the night.

The Cove Motel is on Denman Street. The beach is two minutes away. Our room has two beds, a sitting room and a kitchenette. Mum has brought food from home. For lunch we have soda crackers, cheddar cheese, apples cored and cut into "boats," and sultana cookies. Mum has her tea, I have a Coke. It's not Friday. But I have a Coke. It's warm but good. The room is warm too. The Formica table where we eat lunch is set beneath two big windows.

We watch the lacy curtains pull back and forth with the wind from the open window. We are silent, watching the material breathe so easily. In time, our own breaths match the rhythm.

We go to the beach. The harbour has even more sailboats in it now. We walk at the ocean's edge and squeal when the waves touch the toes of our shoes. Turning, we stop at a popcorn vendor's and buy popcorn. The paper bag is slick with butter, the popcorn, spilling over the top, is hot and delicious.

Back at our room we take off our wet shoes and socks. Mum is pleased that she remembered our slippers. We change into cozy clothes and book-end the couch, our stories in hand. We read in silence.

I could tell her. I could tell her that Dad is coming back. That she won't have to drive a taxi anymore, and we won't have to have another family share the house this autumn, so Mum can train to be a teacher. I can't make my blonde-haired sister come home more often, and none of us are safe from my red-haired sister's claws. My brother likes to laugh, but mostly, he's as angry and sad as Mum. He really misses Dad. I guess I can't fix that, either. I don't even know when, exactly, Dad is coming back. All the same, I should tell her: *We're going to be all right, Mum.*

I start to speak and then look up at my mother's intent reading face. Not just intent but soft. I haven't seen peace on my mother's face in many months.

She looks up, finds my studying eyes, smiles.

"I am going to teach you a game. It's called honeymoon bridge."

Out come the cards and score-pad. I am not good at the game but I like it. It's a grown-up game, like poker, but it's also our game, Mum's and mine. *Trump. Singleton. Bluffing. Suits. Void. One heart.* All these fun new words and ideas. I like to watch her hands when she shuffles and deals the cards. Her movements are tidy. Calm, somehow, too.

We play until dark, eat a peanut butter and banana sandwich, and prepare to sleep in separate beds. I thought we'd share a bed.

"I love you," she says, smiling, "but you kick and thrash in your sleep."

The next morning she is awake before I am and rises quickly. Yesterday is far away. Today is already heavy on her shoulders. She makes tea, packs away the cards and our belongings.

"Your brother," she says—the thin sound of her voice scares me—"I must phone him." She calls my brother. He was worried, Mum tells me, hanging up the receiver. He wants us to come home. We hurry around the room, straightening bed covers and washing and drying our dishes. When we leave, there is nothing to say we were ever in the room.

What in the name of God was I thinking, I hear her mutter.

I am glad we're going home. I need to hear a few slamming doors. People do leave our house, but they come back home too. My blonde-haired sister will be home today, and we'll all have supper together; sometimes she and I sing *Frère Jacques* in rounds when we dry the supper dishes. My red-haired sister still won't be back until tomorrow. My brother won't be sad or mad today, he'll be glad we are back.

Sometimes I think that Dad may not come back. He doesn't really like that cravat on the bureau, and I guess he can buy more aftershave. *Replaceable*. Things. People. I hadn't thought of that before. My stomach returns to its usual twisted place. Then I look at Mum. Even worried, her face isn't as tight as it was yesterday. She touches my cheek.

"We'll be all right, little love," she says. We drive to the house with many doors. We enter through the back door and bring the sound of bells with us.

PERFUME

Kate Braid

She was mother to his six children,
each demanding just the usual
blood and bone. For them she regularly surrendered
a new dress, shoes that wouldn't hurt her bunions so badly,
so Kim could have skates, Linda get glasses.

Once a year on Christmas Eve he expressed
his appreciation by going to the Rexall Drug at the mall
just before closing time to buy her
a bottle of *Poison*, real perfume,
and have it wrapped by the cute blonde at the counter
who flirts and writes a very nice note on the card
he will lay under the tree.

In the morning, after kid gifts are opened
and the fierce shouts of pleasure over trucks and Barbie dolls
subside, it's her turn. The kids look away, knowing
what's in the small box, what dad will say
when she opens it. Her face a little pale, she will wait
a little too long before she looks up.
Real perfume! he will prompt and she will smile
and kiss his cheek *Thank you* as she always does
and he will be disappointed. *My wife
is a cold woman,* he will tell the other.

GERANIUM

Lorri Neilsen Glenn

Face down in the flowerbed this time, whimpering. The others on the bench outside, their permed white curls blinking in the prairie wind, mouths hash marks of disdain. I leave the car running & Allison lifts her into the back seat. A red geranium petal crushed into her temple & those maroon polyester pants of hers with the elasticized waist drooped around a dark stain. God, I hate the smell of geraniums. Sad, sour, reactionary plants. Smug even. *He's been watching me.* She is trying to sit up now, growling. *Hand me that— you don't smoke. Give me one. What are you doing?* Her eyes in the rear view mirror—forty years & they still feel like a slap. *He parks below my window, away from the entrance. That's stalking, you know. He's a nutcase. And no cheques. I have to take him to court again. Not. A. Dime.* I toss the butt out the window; it's made me dizzy. Allison & I will have to call the guys, tell them to feed the kids. Left my scotch on the table when the superintendent called. God, I probably smell just like her. Missed the turn—okay, around the block again. Allison is looking at me: say something. I know—we should say something. *Thirty-eight years, for what? Not a dime. Where the hell are you taking me?* Her face thrust between the front seats, dirt in her hair. I signal to turn & my hand shakes. My sister frowns at me, looks at her. You need some help, Allison starts. *I don't need your help, Missy. You haven't called for months. I don't need anyone's fucking help. I raised you girls, and you turned out just like him. How the hell, I don't know. I should have aborted all of you. Help!* Air rush. The back window rolling down. The door handle: *Help—Over here!* A kid with a skateboard outside the 7-Eleven looks over, then away. The light changes & I move into the intersection. Gravel sound from the open back door, as Allison crawls over the gearbox, a car behind me honking. *Just like him. The both of you. Oh, god. I'm so alone.* The maroon pants, her sensible shoes, sagging white belly, the curb. Brakes. City heat baked into the concrete. Lifting her from the street. Her arms swinging. My hair in her fist. Blood on her chin. My arm wet. A fire truck howling around the corner. Across the street, at the detox centre, a planter of treated wood and stems of bobbing red. Of course. Allison's eyes on me now: And you wonder, she says. You wonder.

Dusk, If That

to my mother, 1921-2007
Leanne Averbach

       Elsewhere
on earth, the shoeless   Pound, pound
Dust drinking up bloody feet   Even I have seen
rough alley, seen boulevard, dead shoes lone, telling
in the road   I've dwelt years in notorious
intersections of thought, and some danger

       But I'm safe now
and it's dusk, if that   Yet night burns
like a hobo—hands asleep on the rails   Something
going on in things grows indistinct   Mother:
vanished beginning   my tender source —

      On the wisteria, sun spark
And this salt face   Sky is tufting its feminine
hour, white on rose   Behind, the moon   smudged
      as *errata*

      I am the mare
moving dumbly up the tracks   I am the mouth
eating your words   Biting off
the sentence I'm no longer in: Daughter.

SURVIVAL PART TWO:
ON BEING A NEW MOTHER IN A NEW LAND

Marsha Lederman

It was about ten months after my mother died that I stopped being able to use a public bathroom. Every time I approached one, often at a place like a shopping mall, I could hear my mother's voice. "I need the bathroom." In her final few years of life, the bathroom was something she *needed*; a request soaked in vulnerability. It made me uncomfortable during her life, and, since her death, the memory of it has me driving home from malls at a clipped pace, her anxious statement amplified now that I understand just how fragile she was—some of those requests coming weeks, even days, before her death.

I suppose it is a natural thing for children to be uncomfortable with their parents' vulnerability. These are the people who provide for us in every way, who tell us and give us everything. From our earliest memories, they are there to guide, fix, and scold. They are all-powerful and all-knowing. Maybe the phrasing of the bathroom request somehow echoed an earlier shock—that first time we stump our parents with a question. What, they don't know everything?

For me, my parents' vulnerability came to light very early. I was brought up with my family's tragic history hovering over and under us in the house, presented as matter-of-fact truth.

Why don't I have grandparents, like my friends do?

Because your grandparents were gassed to death. They were told they were going to have a shower but gas came out instead.

Oh.

This kind of blatant answer to a five-year-old's question could potentially do some damage, I imagine. I'm sure it has. But at the time, it felt, well, normal to have such a freaky family history. It was all I knew.

My parents grew up Jewish in Poland, my mother in a city called Radom, my father in Lodz. My mother remembers the start of the Second World War and the immediate personal fall-out: when the Germans marched into Poland on September 1, 1939, it meant for her that the first day of school was cancelled. She was crushed. The effects, ultimately, on both my parents were of course far more devastating. My father escaped a death decree in the ghetto and spent the war hiding his identity in Germany, working as a farmhand and pretending to be a Catholic Pole. My mother spent years in concentration and labour camps, before being sent off on a death march in the final hours of the war. Their parents and most of their siblings were murdered.

My mother was 14 when the war began and 20 when it ended. In my teens, when I complained of some teenage horror, like having a boyfriend break up with me, or not having the right jeans, or not being allowed to spend more than $400 on my prom dress, my mother reminded me that she had no prom, no boyfriends, no shoes, even. It was Auschwitz for her.

My mother was robbed of being a teenager. And I, as a teenager, was robbed of a cherished teenaged tradition: complaining.

I complained about that too, probably to my girlfriends at the time and, eventually, to a therapist. It's odd that, while I could barely face the horrors that had happened to my mother during the Holocaust because my grief and anger were too powerful, I was unable to feel much if any compassion for what happened to her after that.

It's only since her death that I have started contemplating what my mother must have faced as a young mother herself, and, ultimately, as a not-so-young mother to me.

I picture her now, a brand new arrival to Canada in 1951. She had a husband, a little girl, some money stashed in a suitcase, and a set of Rosenthal dishes. She could not speak English. She had no skills, no education. She lived in an attic apartment in Toronto's Kensington market. The flat was cramped and hot, and the landlady was mean.

My mother, Gucia, had no mother to teach her how to breastfeed or make baby food or change a diaper ... or to cope. When another daughter came along later that decade, perhaps by then my mother was able to get by in English and wipe a baby's behind with the best of them, and she had likely perfected her chicken soup and apple cake too. But I figure by then the shock of her great losses must have worn off, and the self-awareness must have crept in, and I imagine she was left with the gripping loneliness of having no mother to turn to with technical—and big picture—queries, no-one to leave her daughters with for a night out or even an hour of respite, no one to call up on the phone and ask things young mothers tend to wonder about. Was I like this? What did you do when I cried for three hours straight? When did I start sleeping through the night? What were my first words?

The Nazis robbed my mother of the opportunity to ask these questions. I hardly think she, at the age of 14, would have thought to ask her own mother for such intimate details—if such questions were even asked then. Surely none of this would have mattered as the Second World War closed in on them and as, one night, Gucia's mother was dragged off in a cattle car to the gas chamber at Treblinka. The prayers—and questions—went unanswered.

Half-a-world away and more than half-a-century later, I too feel robbed of the opportunity to ask my mother these questions. But there are no Nazis to blame in my story. Just myself. I never got around to it.

When my mother died suddenly, on a vacation in Florida, I was shocked, devastated, and deeply sad. But, at the *shiva*, the week of mourning which follows the funeral, I did have the presence of mind to look around at my friends and family, and wonder about the deaths my young mother had experienced. She lost her parents, her brother, her friends, her home, her shoes, every little possession, every dream. And she, unlike me, did not have the luxury of mourning.

It was losing my mother that made me think about her loss of her mother. And, later, it was becoming a stepmother to young children that had me thinking about how my mother had dealt with parenting, in the days before it became a section in the bookstore. She had nothing to go by, nobody to ask, no model to base her decisions on. Her parents had done everything they could for their children. But the definition of "everything they could" went in one generation from stealing a couple of pieces of bread for them to choosing the right piano teacher.

And so the stumping-the-parents moment came early for me. As a child, if I brought homework to the kitchen table, it was not my mother who was able to help me, but one of my older sisters. My mother in fact was going to school at the same time I was, taking night classes at a local high school. She read the daily-delivered newspaper not because she wanted to keep up with the politics of the land, but because she wanted to practice her English. When she had to write a note to my teacher, or even fill out a reply card for a wedding or bar mitzvah invitation, she wrote a draft, I proofread it, and then she painstakingly copied the corrected sentences onto the notepaper or the RSVP request.

There was a story my mother used to love to tell. When I was in public school, maybe in grade three or four, the mild-mannered principal who had the unfortunate name of Mr. Seuss (luckily he did not have his PhD) invited the parents of the students in my grade to an afternoon meeting. It was at this meeting that he announced that the school was no longer going to be accelerating students; there would be no more skipping of grades. At this news, some of the parents (all mothers) were apoplectic. No more skipping of grades? Why now? Why should their children be robbed of this opportunity? My mother, of course, was silent; embarrassed, perhaps, of her European accent, but more likely unwilling to complain about this decree. She sat quietly and witnessed the uproar around her. Until Mr. Seuss shut his angry mothers down. "If anyone was going to skip a grade," he interrupted, "it would be Marsha Lederman." As my mother tells it, all eyes in the room turned to her and narrowed as if to say 'that *greener* is the mother of the smartest kid in the class?' ("greener" being a term used in those days to describe new immigrants, especially Jewish post-war arrivals). I think it may have been my mother's proudest moment. None of the A-plusses I brought home over the years compared.

My mother did not work after I was born and she did not drive. My father made the money, invested it, and paid the bills. My mother contributed to the household in a different way: she cooked and cleaned and tried not to spend extravagantly. My father wouldn't let her take driving lessons. It wasn't as if he had more power than her; it was just that he was protective and wanted to take care of her himself. He promised he would drive her everywhere. And, generally, he did.

When my father died—also suddenly and also on a trip—I inherited his car, his cheque book, and the role of constant companion to my mother. I was 18.

I have complained bitterly at times about being robbed of having a fully-parented upbringing; that it was me who had to do the parenting from a too-young age, as my fifty-something mother struggled with the sudden death of her husband. She was depressed and unprepared to manage the household. Without her driver's license, she could not even buy the groceries. It all fell to me. It seems incredible to me now that I would have complained about this. Because since my mother's death, it is this very thought—that I drove her to the supermarket, helped her at the bank, and especially that I kept her company—that gives me my only comfort, as I wade through this suffocating loss. Maybe, in the tiniest of ways, I gave my mother some of that mothering she lost so early in her own life.

I never thought to ask my mother the questions she could not ask her mother. What was my first word? When did I start sleeping through the night? What was she feeling when she became pregnant with me at the age of 40? When she gave birth to me on a hot July morning? What was she like, as a young mother? I cannot ask her now. All I can do it look for clues. In my sisters and myself.

When my mother was alive, I viewed her as weak. She managed to survive the Holocaust, yes, but she needed me to write her thank-you notes and pay her taxes and open her jars of pickles. I didn't understand that her strength lay in the struggles she faced, and in her refusal to let them stop her from living her life, having her children, and even in asking us, at times, for help.

Now with the cruel perspective of time and her death, I am able to recognize my mother's strength. After all she suffered, she did not give up. She did not collapse into victimhood. She did not seek refuge in a bottle of vodka or a prescription for Valium or in an insane asylum. She chose, instead, to pick up and start again. Marry and move to Canada and learn English and raise children and attend our parent-teacher nights and entertain our petty demands and laugh with her friends on the telephone. She was able to survive her losses and move on to conquer the mundane. And even though I can't ask her now about toilet training or birthday parties or cures for a childhood fever, I can look back and learn so much, just by doing that: remembering everything she did for me. Beginning with surviving.

THE DIRTY BLONDE IN THE YELLOW PAJAMAS

Deb Loughead

Every now and then our mother holds up her hands for my sister and me to inspect, a swollen-knuckle testimony to the years she spent scrubbing. She never points with her index finger any more; it's grown crooked, she claims, from having twisted rags for so long. She points with her middle finger, the only straight one left, to emphasize a point. This once elicited hoots of laughter from the grandchildren before they grew accustomed to the habit.

Growing up in our protected 1950s enclave in west-end Toronto, in a neighbourhood known as Swansea, my sister and I were shielded by a mommy who staved off germs with her compulsive cleanliness. Some days, it seemed as if we saw more of her backside than the rest of her. When she wasn't cleaning, she was cooking or mending or doing the laundry. Or cleaning up after our grandfather (we lived in his house, after all) who had a penchant for spitting in the kitchen sink and leaving a trail of crumbs and dirty dishes around whenever he cooked. The only upside to her fastidious domestic habits was her technique for distracting us when she was busy.

That was by telling us stories.

My younger sister was the quiet and serene child. She didn't squawk or fuss, could amuse herself with building blocks for an hour or more. She wasn't stubborn, she was malleable. But I learned quickly if you're malleable, you don't get stories. And so I made noise, rattled and clattered wherever I went, rode my tricycle in furious circles around the living and dining room, never stayed put unless Popeye or Mighty Mouse was on TV. During one of her scarce spare moments, my mother would sit and read to me. But other than my books and cartoon heroes, only her stories could rivet me to the spot for a considerable length of time; it was my mother's secret weapon.

My life of stories started in the high chair, where my mother could trap me while she was down on her knees scrubbing. The storytelling graduated to lunchtime at the kitchen table, to car rides anywhere, to whenever and wherever my sister and I were alone with her and she had a rapt, if not trapped, audience.

As she related her tales, embellishing them with more details the older we got, we gradually became privy to the fact that our mother's childhood was distinctly different from our own. And even though she grew up during the Depression era, she made those years sound vividly bucolic, enchanting even. At least they sounded enchanting to the two of us, but her rambling narratives had an underlying wisp of regret to them that confused us.

No one else who lived on Ottawa's west side had chickens, horses and a barn in their backyards. No one else had a father who pounded on an anvil in the yard or a mother who only wore black and grey. No one else got a ride to school in a horse-drawn wagon, and I could never understand why she'd always buried herself under the hay so that none of her friends would see her. I envied her, would have loved the novelty, but my mother didn't want attention drawn to her living circumstances. Her enduring recollections of that horse and wagon, that farmyard ambience, proved that it had been one of her biggest hang-ups, a symbol of their *habitant* roots. It made them look like backwards country bumpkins.

Make no mistake. She's always had, probably even more so as she's aged, the fondest memories of growing up in the '30s. My grandmother kept her five children clean and well-fed; even in the depths of the Depression years there was always sufficient food on the table. But once, when a boyfriend was kissing Mom goodnight on the front porch and told her that he smelled horse shit, her perfunctory response was: *I don't*. And she always liked to remind us that the house she grew up in was never quite tidy, the floors unfinished planks, the furniture old-fashioned by the standards of the day, steel beds with scratchy horse blankets, wooden kitchen chairs, no phone or hot water.

As she unwound her endless spools of stories, it was as though our mother were trying to make sense of her life, inadvertently dragging my sister and me along on the soul-searching journey. We learned what kind of a child she was, the rebellious streak that endures today, how she got the strap nearly every week in grade five for defying the nuns. Maybe she thought that the focus on her wayward behaviour would distract attention from everything else that she considered disquieting about her life.

To her credit she withheld some of her stories until we were old enough to assimilate them in a positive way and wouldn't try to mimic her. And she saved the tales about how she challenged the rules of the Catholic Church by wearing lipstick and shorts, and necking with boys, until we were old enough to decide for ourselves how that information should be translated. She even told us about how she met our dad while she was hanging out the window of a boarding house in downtown Toronto back in 1950, flirting with some mechanics in a laneway. He threw a note up to her asking her out for a date. And to his friends he referred to her as 'the dirty blonde in the yellow pajamas.' Huh? This gutsy girl and young woman she was always describing couldn't possibly be the same woman who was our mother now.

A year after moving permanently to Toronto, the feisty French Canadian girl from Ottawa married into an extremely foreign Polish culture. Deep in her heart she thought she was doing the right thing when she began to fulfill everyone's expectations by becoming a good wife, mother and daughter-in-law. If she couldn't blend, wouldn't conform in her childhood, broke rules to be distinctive, then she would try her best to do it now. She was probably following the *Father Knows Best* pop culture archetype of the time; a family with two daughters who were always perfectly clean and neat, and a spotless home that people would take note of in a positive way (even though my grandmother once remarked in a whispered aside that our mother could catch the dust before it fell).

She tried her best to meet the standard, to create that atmosphere of perfection in her own home by scrubbing away everything she wanted to forget about the parts of her childhood that had made her feel ashamed. There was a downside to projecting this image though, because by over-compensating in this way she had to quell so much of her true nature, so much of what we had gleaned from her stories about that irrepressible person she used to be.

Our parents were never apart, never led singular and distinctive lives of their own. Our mother, an elementary school teacher who "retired" when I was born, had to wear dresses on Sunday, couldn't read a book or even knit if our father was in the same room with her because he required her complete attention. She could never tell off-colour jokes, could never act foolish and impetuous in public, always had to maintain her wifely veneer. And if that buried feistiness dared to rear its ugly head, she was sure to be reprimanded when they were alone. For some reason she settled for this. She tolerated it.

And what if we hadn't been privy to her stories? What if she hadn't begun the tradition of sharing them that she continues even to this day, if reminiscing hadn't been part of her agenda? We wouldn't know what she was really all about, might be in danger of making the same mistakes ourselves.

If she hadn't shared her stories, then we would have known her only as a mother who'd conformed to rigid housekeeping standards in an era when it was expected, if not demanded by society. She missed the Cuban Missile Crisis because she was busy painting the living room, couldn't understand why all her friends were calling her up and sobbing their anxieties; she listened, receiver in one hand, wet paintbrush in the other, then quickly said good-bye.

Lucky for us, though, time spent with our mother was always a sort of running commentary that made us cognizant of her deepest thoughts, of what she rejoiced in or regretted the most. Over the years we've been slowly snapping on the corners of her puzzle, filling in the centre, closing up the edges, pressing everything into place. We had to be mature women, mothers ourselves, before we could even begin to see the complete picture, to get a feeling for "what lies beneath" the woman who was our mother.

We learned that, under all the wife-and-mother trappings, she buried a vital, intelligent woman with a surplus of strength and passion that she was never given the opportunity to use. Yet perhaps these hallmarks of her spirit provided the very attributes that she required to help her conform, to help her endure the narrow and limited expectations of a woman living in that era.

After our father died in 1986, our mother spent five years grieving. That was a long time to grieve, but as she continued to share her multitude of stories, some of the reasons emerged. Once she finally finished mourning him and the predictable routine she'd grown so accustomed to, she had a revelation, an epiphany of sorts that she was at first reluctant to acknowledge: She finally felt liberated. She didn't have to answer to anyone, ever again. That revelation was a difficult one to absorb and digest—until she could finally get past the guilt.

If she didn't rebel then, our mother is doing it now, displaying that fiery passion she stifled for so long. And if she hadn't related her stories, how would we possibly understand her distinctively non-matriarchal behaviour as she aged, her aberration from all that is grey and doting and stoic and serene? There are still issues cluttering up her head that she will never be able to reconcile. But there is also a sense of complacency because she endured and lived to share the story.

Our mother hasn't buried herself in the shadows of her hardships and misfortunes; she's demonstrated a tenaciousness that has buoyed her up over the years. She still revels in her life, as if 'the dirty blonde in the yellow pajamas' has come back in the flesh to pick up where she left off so long ago. Recently she told me that now she finally feels truly content. She lives in a small but perfect house, has everything she needs in the way of mental and spiritual fulfilment with her church volunteer work, her passion for reading and the study of history, a close-knit family and enduring friendships that she continues to nurture. She confessed, with a soupçon of guilt, that she has never felt more at ease, at last, in her own skin. Then she offered a complacent, yet an almost apologetic smile, because she knows how much she's revealed about what lies beneath.

As I close in on 35 years as a wife and mother, my own index finger is becoming a bit crooked now. Maybe it's from all the time I spent scribbling stories and poems with a pen before I began using my computer more than twenty years back. Or maybe it's just hereditary.

It's certainly not from scrubbing.

BIRTH MOTHER: PHONE CALL

Susan Helwig

For nine months, your Voice, the only voice
I ran when you ran
slept when you slept
heard you pass water, break wind, burp

Now the pale words through thirty years of ocean
hardly make sense
where are the teary scenes
counselling prepared us for?

How *are* you?
then repeated, as if transposed to a different
key
How are *you*?

and *Have a great day!*
again, *Have a great day!*

though it is night for you, morning for me
strange, the song your speech makes;
fitting, the phone's display

—*unknown caller*—

In My Blood

Shauna Butterwick

A long line of pearls, irregular, not cultured. After a while,
the surface flakes away, revealing their dime store origin.
They say the devil's in the details, say that you can tell a wolf
in sheep's clothing, and not to reap before you sow. They
say she had a mind of her own, was good with words,
but never played by the book. They met after the war,
he fell in love at first sight, she decided it was
getting late, so why not. A civil ceremony, no white
for this virgin. Set up house above the shop
in a small, small town.

A long line of secondhand laundry flapping in the breeze,
snapping in the current, then frozen stiff and stubborn.
They say it's an ill wind that blows no one any good. Better
to have the wind at your back, in your sails, to know its direction.
They say it always blew in our town west to east, spilling
down mountains, across foothills. Later, they put up windmills,
a row of white herons on Cowley Ridge. We came from two doors
down, beside the house with the un-mown lawn, a field
of grasses where cats stalked, stayed low, tails twitching,
whiskers trembling, waiting for birds. They got away, just in time.

A long line of small moments added on like beads, most dull,
unpolished. A few gems among the gravel. They say life's like that,
one day after another, one thing after the next. One wonders.
They say I'm like my mother who could turn stones into fire, make
something out of nothing. Oats into bread, onions into pies, words
into missiles. She got pregnant at 43. When she lost that child,
her heart broke. We stayed with my cousins, not knowing her grief
while she took to her bed, washed down little blue pills
with skim milk, and later, wine.

A long line of words (his and hers), like cards in a deck
waiting to be played. They say: keep them close to your chest.
Give nothing away. Don't wear your heart on your sleeve.
They say I look like my sister, except that I don't. We are not
like our mother: too much, too loud. Not refined. She ate
like a bird, kept budgies to share her grief and loss.
No grandchildren, no houses, fences, no worries.
We eat with gusto, too fast, keep cats who catch birds, keep
lists to cross off. We make our own way, walk our own path,
not noticing we're on the same road, caught in the same bind.

A long line of four-door cars. Waiting for trains to cross,
ferries to arrive, lights to change. They say you reap what you sow,
weather the storm and take what comes. They wonder what
will happen to me, given the weather, the traffic, family history.
We watched as she left us, her mind slipping little by little.
She'd come back on occasion, and I'd see glimpses of her blue eyes
flashing, as if she were listening. I dream of her now: we're
at a party, she is happy to see me, surprised by my tears,
telling me everything's going to be fine.

GODMOTHER

Sylvia Hamilton

This is Godmother, this is Mom
and that's me in the middle.
We were in New Glasgow—Second African United Baptist Church.
Look at us! We look alike—sort of. I mean, we're
about the same height. See the shoulder lines.
Look at those clothes. I had on a suit. After all, it was
the Women's Institute service. I think I had to speak …
the suit, yeah, but no hat. Should have had one though,
that haircut—ooh cut too short, bad cut, I mean how tough
is it to cut an Afro? He's a good barber everyone said—
so good the man gave me a bald spot in the back of my head,
then tried to cover it up.

Godmother. Godmother.
Her name was Eva—Eva Agnes, my dad's sister.
Lived just down the hill from us, so close Mom could call down
or she could yell up—*Sista-in-law Marie!*
We'd run down with something, and back up the rocky hill
again—many times a day.

When I was too big for the annual Christmas underwear—
*you can always use underwear, remember
to put on clean underwear every day, you never know
where you'll end up—what if you were in an accident?
get to the hospital and have on dirty underwear—
shame shame.*

China tea cups became the gift. *Go in that China cabinet
and pick out one—let me see it first 'fore you run off with it.
Save it for your Hope Chest. You need a Hope Chest.*

Was that hope you never get married, or hope to get married,
or hope you get a chest some day?

I took the French blue and white one with the two chips
near the handle.

Don't remember any anyone talking about Hope Chests
except Godmother. Don't remember any anyone being able
to turn back an eyelid with a wooden match stick.

Playing softball in the rocky, dusty clearing meant that
someone before the end of the game would have bits of dirt
lodged in an eye. Mostly you kept playing and it'd work itself out.
But those stubborn, nasty bits were a problem
*blow on it! take the corner of your
shirt, spit on it make it wet, roll it tight tight
dab at it   that'll   work ...*

No, no. Nothing worked. Silence.
Everyone knew what had to be done.

*I'm not going.
I'm not going down there.
She ain't gonna do that to me.
It look so awful when she does it!
You see all the insides of your eye.
Woaah, oohhh   nooooo
Come on. You got to.
What's worse, her turning up your
eye, or being blind the rest of your life?
That bit of rock can scratch your eye
and you won't see nothing, ever ever again.*

Down the rocky path to Aunt Eva's.

You go knock, she's your Godmother.
Maybe she's not even home yet.
Just knock.
Godmother? You home?
Who's it?
It's me.
Who got dirt this time?

We never figured out how she always knew it was us.

Silently we'd walk in the back door.
Solemn, almost like the pretend funerals we used
to have for inch worms and anything else we found dead
(or killed, like the small green snakes in the blueberry patch).

The sound of the match striking the box or
stove stop jarred us from our quiet.
A burnt match works best.

Sit here between my legs on this stool
hold your head back   look down but don't shut
your eyes hold still now stop jiggling around

She pulls the eyelid away from
the eye by pinching her two fingers together
pulls the lid out   quickly inserts the wooden match stick
on top of the lid, turns   she dabs with something, or pours water
or ... but the thing is gone.

It's gone. May be it was just scared away.

Get on outta here you fellas be more careful.
I got no time to do this everyday.
I would go for visits.
She'd serve tea in her china tea cups.
Lots of milk, lumps of sugar.

I had to drink it—she was my Godmother.
She baked apple pie with nutmeg,
topped it with fresh cream.

Today I drink tea, but no milk please.
She tried to teach me how to care
for African Violets,

I remember   I try.

THE FORWARD LOOK

THE GIRLS IN THE SNAPSHOT

for my mother
Janet Barkhouse

Both lie on their bellies, laugh into the camera,
a Brownie Box, just outside
the frame. Green grass shows through last year's
stubble. You can see it's green though the photo is sepia, can see
the girls' glossy hair is brown, their eyes hazel.
One of the girls lies almost flat,
only her face up—she's reaching
forward with a rough alder stick in her hand, the stick
she just this second touched to the shutter release.
She's seventeen. It's a birthday picnic,
a sparkling May 3, 1930, Uncle Scott's pasture
up the North Mountain. Salt tickles the air—
at the foot of the cliff behind them
waves whisper ashore, ashore.

Later they'll build a fire, cook bacon on that stick,
talk about final exams, *Provincials*, last days
in the Big Part of their two-room school.
Peer into flames that flare and smoke—
they've never been anywhere
but ordinary *here*; thrilling *there* awaits them.

Hold these girls in the cup of your hand, skin
thin as the paper they lie on. Your hand
is old, you know
what they don't. Hold them
tender and sepia green.

THE FORWARD LOOK

Janice Acton

"Holy Cow! The new Chryslers are going to be at Gage's Garage tomorrow. Can I go?"

My mother looked up from a tray of freshly-baked cinnamon buns whose doughy crevasses oozed melted butter, brown sugar and raisins. She wiped her hands on a tea towel.

"We'll see. Tell Davie you'll call him back."

"Mom says I have to call you back." I leaned into the receiver of our wall crank phone and listened while my best friend, Davie, stressed the urgency of us going to town to see the swank new line of 1957 Forward Look Chryslers.

"Yeah, okay, I'll try," I said and hung up.

The annual arrival of the new line of cars in Loamtown—our dusty little Saskatchewan town of 475 souls—was always a red-letter day. The unveiling of the cars gave farmers in the outlying area an excuse to come to town. After shopping and then milling about in front of the post office, folks would drift over to Gage's Garage to run their fingers over the plush leather seats of the new cars. With a price tag of $5,359, this would be the closest most would ever come to owning one of these beauties—unless they won the car raffle.

"Can't you drive me?" I pleaded to my mother who was thrusting another tray of buns into the oven. The dial on our T. Eaton's Moffat

Range glowed rosy pink with anticipation. As a nine- year-old living miles from town, I was dependent on the schedule of adults.

"I'm afraid I can't, dear. Tomorrow is my first day of work, remember? And your father won't be back in time."

"Oh darn." I slouched, elbows on our Formica table. Since the fall, my father had been attending classes in Regina, sixty miles away, in order to get his senior matriculation. His high school correspondence courses had not prepared him for the rigours of the new math and sciences he would need at university so he struggled with them and often had to stay late to re-do his chemistry labs.

My mother was intent upon getting the ham and mashed potatoes on the table so she listened to my lament with only half an ear. My mother was a pragmatist. She faced challenges and adversity by anchoring herself to the practical, planning tomorrow's meals out of today's leftovers and buying our clothes a size too large so that we could grow into them.

"You can probably get a ride with Davie's dad."

"It's not fair."

Indeed, nothing seemed fair to me these days. After years of endless discussions, my parents had finally concluded our farm would never be economically viable. In order to get ahead, they decided we would need to move off our farm during the winter months. In the spring my father would return to the farm to plant the crops while my mother and sister and I would live in town, travelling back and forth to the farm as often as possible. Initially we would move into Loamtown and then eventually to Saskatoon where my father could attend university. The lynchpin of this multi-phase plan was my mother getting a job. Fortuitously, the CCF government had just created a new health district in our area and my mother was hired as its Public Health nurse.

My mother's decision to work outside the home was met by scepticism and criticism on every front, not only by traditionally-minded friends and neighbours but also by some members of her own family—including me. However, no matter how much I resisted or disagreed with the plan of moving off the farm, I had no power to alter the changing course of our lives.

∽

Next morning the regional nursing supervisor, Miss Hopkins, arrived to drive my mother to the Public Health office in Melville, thirty miles away. She was dressed in the Public Health nurse's uniform, a navy blue dress with serviceable pockets and a starched white collar.

"Hello, Janice," she said, offering me an adult-like handshake. "I've heard a lot about you."

I immediately liked her. I didn't feel the judgment I picked up from a lot of adults when they scrutinized my tomboy clothes and close-cropped hair.

"I understand this is a pretty big day," she said by way of breaking the ice.

I cocked my head inquisitively.

"The car show is in town?"

I nodded. "Yeah ... this afternoon."

"What's the best car this year?" Miss Hopkins asked.

I couldn't believe this woman with grey hair and granny tie-up shoes was interested in cars.

"Chrysler's Forward Look," I said, pulling a newspaper clipping out of my blue jeans pocket and thrusting it into Miss Hopkins' hand.

Drive with the Forward Look!

*The long, low Chrysler for 1957 is an automobile
of breathless beauty. Every rakish angle, from its
eager, forward-thrust front profile to its dashing
upswept tail fins, from hooded headlights to boldly
slanted taillights, has the look of beauty.*

Miss Hopkins raised her eyebrows. "I'd certainly like a car like that."

"I bought two tickets for the car raffle because our old car is falling apart."

"Well, I hope you have the winning ticket," Miss Hopkins said. "But maybe you'll get a new car now that your mother is going to work." I was never very good at hiding my feelings. I looked down at my scuffed cowboy boots.

She leaned over to make eye contact. "Don't you want your mother to work?"

"I ... I ... guess so ... but ..."

"But," she prodded, "you aren't so sure because ..."

"... because she's the only one," I blurted out, betraying my feelings of hurt and powerlessness.

"Oh I see." Miss Hopkins sat back. "But do you know how important your mother's work will be? She's going to set up polio clinics so that people don't ever get that terrible disease again."

I pictured my aunt lying in an iron lung machine at the hospital, and the girl next door to my grandparents who wore an ugly brace and could only run by hopping on her good leg.

"Your mother tells me you will be able to take care of yourself on the nights she works late. She says you're an excellent cook, is that right?"

"I guess so. I can make Minute Rice and fried Spam. And Welsh rarebit. That's when I pour a can of Campbell's cheese soup over toast."

"Well, that's very creative," Miss Hopkins said enthusiastically. Then she took my hands in hers. "Some day you'll be very proud of your mother because she has the courage to do what nobody else is doing. And you're right. She's not like any other mom. That makes her very special."

∞

That afternoon, I swung into town with Davie and his dad, Jordie, in their emerald green 1956 Dodge Custom Royal. Through some cruel twist of fate, Jordie's land just south of ours regularly produced bumper crops so he was always able to buy the most up-to-date cars the moment they rolled off the conveyor belt.

Since we had two hours to kill before the raffle Davie and I decided to hang out at the bowling alley in the back of Al Tarpolski's barber shop. But nothing much was happening there, so we meandered down Main Street, Davie drinking his Orange Crush, and me chewing on a licorice pipe. We wandered over to Rexall Drugs and spun the rotating comic book shelf to see what looked good. I picked out a Lone Ranger comic. The cash register ka-chinged as the balding druggist, Mr. Hart, took my dime.

"I hear your mother is going to be the new Public Health nurse." He peered down at me. It didn't seem like a question, so I just nodded and then lit out the door.

Next we stopped at the Co-op Store in order to check the time. We had to elbow our way around shelves crammed with blue jeans, dish towels, long underwear and aprons in order to find the clock. Through the mountain of clothing I discerned the muffled voices of our neighbours, Elsie and Sandra.

"... such a shame ... the girls are still so young ..."

"... don't know what the poor man thinks of it ..."

I yanked Davie towards the door and stormed down the sidewalk.

"You bugged about something?" he said, bewildered.

"Yeah. Everybody thinks my mom shouldn't go to work."

"So, how come she's going to work?"

I pushed Davie up against the wall of Kruger's Blacksmith shop. "She's going to work to fight polio," I declared as if my mother were going off to the Crusades. "So that nobody ever gets that terrible disease again."

"Okay, okay. Don't get your shirt in a knot." Davie wriggled away.

My stomach churned, just like the time I overheard Mrs. Pickfield talking about me to my mother.

"Don't you sometimes wonder if there isn't something a little wrong with her?" she asked, just because she didn't think I should play hockey or wear a cowboy hat.

My mother had replied without missing a beat: "Of course not. She's just a normal active girl."

It was none of Mrs. Pickfield's bees-wax how I dressed, so I figured it was nobody's business but my mother's if she wanted to work. And yet, my feelings betrayed me. While I supported my mother's right to make this decision, deep in my heart I struggled to understand why we had to be "different" from everybody else who seemed to fit 100% into the grid of farming life.

⟳

"... and the winner is ..." Davie and I squeezed into the crowd in front of the garage just as Charlie Gage was dipping his hand into the raffle box. Excitement surged through the crowd.

"The winner is ..." Charlie opened the scrap of paper and dramatically hesitated like the host on the $64,000 Question show: "... Billie Koslowski!"

For a moment, people stood stunned. Then Mrs. Koslowski, the town's telephone operator, pushed through the crowd with her freckled four-year-old son, Billie, in tow.

"Thank you, thank you," Mrs. Koslowski blurted, her face flushed with joy. "I bought the ticket in Billie's name."

Charlie thrust his grease-stained paw out to shake Billie's hand. "Well, I'll be darned. Congratulations, Billie."

A general hubbub of guffawing and back-slapping ensued. "For gosh sake." "Well, doesn't that take the cake!"

"Attention," Charlie hollered as people began to drift away. "The Loamtown Booster Club has raised $1714. Thanks to you, we'll be in that new curling rink before you know it!"

⌒

"Sorry you didn't win the car," Davie said as we walked back towards the Co-op store.

"Aw, it's okay." I shrugged. "I've never won anything, except for a Quaker Oats contest once. But they sent me a majorette's baton because I was a girl, even though I told them I wanted a football."

"Jeez, that's too bad," Davie said.

"Hey, there's my mom." I yelled: "Mom!" and ran towards the familiar figure. She was standing beside a parked car and she was dressed in a tailored navy blue dress with serviceable pockets and a white collar.

"Hi, dear, how was the car show?"

"It was okay," I stated matter-of-factly. "I didn't win the car raffle."

"Never mind," she said, smiling. "We'll get by without it."

Then I heard Davie murmuring, "wow," as he dragged his finger along the chrome trim of the royal blue 1957 Chevrolet beside which my mother was standing.

My mouth dropped open. "Is this your car?"

"That's right," my mother said nodding. "I have this car for my work because I need to drive to so many places. Of course, it's not fancy like those new Chryslers. Now, do you want to come home with me or with Davie's dad?"

"Come on," I yelled at Davie. "Let's get a ride with my mom."

SOMETHING DIFFERENT

Frances Boyle

My mother tells me she dreamed
of something different.

A shimmering
movie-saturated past
of tinkling parties, smart
cocktail dresses, little hats
with veils. Conversation,
laughter, picnics and drives
through the countryside
frozen in photos or blurred
in memory montage.

She speaks of the opera
(the grey squirrel wrap
I used to love to stroke, slippery
feel of a strand of pearls, hush
in velvet seats before the music).
I flip through stories of cafes and quests
pressed in a musty book
static pictures of the Met
cardboard sets and costumes
so fake they make me mock.

Saturday afternoons, I plead
for her to turn off the radio.
A part of her I don't recognize.
—the shrieking of the arias—
her dreams an era already creaky
to my teenage certainty.
The life she has
is not the life she wanted,
not the one she wants for me but

I want a life of my own making,
textures of thrift store silk
and rough suede, scent of musk
or patchouli. Dreams of strong arms,
warm kisses. We both dream
it seems, of heroes.

THE ALIEN CORN

Pam Thomas

Perhaps the self-same song that found a path
Through the sad heart of Ruth, when, sick for home,
She stood in tears amid the alien corn;
> Keats, *Ode to a Nightingale*

My mother was a child prodigy on the violin. She was born in 1920 in the quiet Transylvanian town of Kezdivasarhely. It was a difficult time to be Hungarian in Transylvania, which had just been handed over to Romania after the First World War and the break up of the Austro-Hungarian Empire. The Hungarians, who overnight became an ethnic minority in their own country, were fiercely patriotic and defiant. My sisters and I, westerners to the core, grew up believing that all Romanians were evil. 'Never let a Romanian kiss your hand,' my mother told us, 'because he'll bite your fingers. Or at best you'll come away without your rings.'

When my mother was five, she saw her handsome soldier cousin playing his violin, and she begged to have one too. She started lessons soon after, and gave her first public performance at the age of seven. Her teacher, recognizing a precocious talent, arranged for her little pupil to play for Emil Telmanyi who was giving a concert nearby. On his advice, my mother left Transylvania with her parents to study the violin at the Franz Liszt Academy in Budapest. She was eight years old.

What was clear to us from the few stories she chose to tell of her childhood was the intense pressure she'd felt, as a little girl amongst adults, trying to cope with the strict curriculum and expectations of excellence at the Academy, where Bartók and Kodaly were at the height of their fame, and knowing how much her parents had sacrificed for her sake. If she did badly, and her patrons withdrew their support, the family would starve. It was during the Great Depression and the various menial jobs her father found were never secure.

'Did you do well, today?' he asked her anxiously every evening as soon as she got home. 'Did you do all they told you to do?' She absorbed a fear of failure into the marrow of her bones. Being a star carried a heavy price.

My mother told us little more of her personal life in Hungary, choosing instead to speak in general and romantic terms of a pre-war Budapest that was remote and unreal to us. She spoke of skating on the Danube in winter, where old women wrapped in shawls roasted chestnuts in little burners on the ice. She told us of servant girls promenading with their beaux on Sunday afternoons, wearing heavily embroidered blouses, and skirts so filled with starched petticoats that they stood out almost horizontally. Hungarian men, she said, danced the *czárdás* and were brilliant and courageous horsemen. We pictured them, with their large moustaches, galloping over the great Hungarian Plains, wearing black hats and waistcoats and wide, white flowing trousers over black boots. These descendants of Attila the Hun were invariably brave and handsome. My mother spoke in sweeping, hyperbolic generalizations, presenting a fairy-tale, one-dimensional country. The real Hungary, when we were small in the 1950s, had disappeared behind the Iron Curtain. It could have been on Mars. All we knew about her parents (she never called them our grandparents) was that her mother had died when she was twelve, and her father had died in the war. When her mother died my mother felt that the last protective barrier between her and the world had been removed. She never felt safe again, and she developed a single-minded instinct for self-preservation that she never lost.

In 1938, unaware of the war clouds gathering over Europe, my mother sailed to America for her first concert tour. Young, beautiful and full of promise, she was on the cusp of a brilliant career. She was also anxious and lonely, and very homesick as she faced this new, alien world. She had no idea that half a century would pass before she would go back home.

Halfway through her tour she met and married a young American writer. It was a brief courtship. She was living with some distant Hungarian relatives whom she disliked, and being a woman who liked to get her own way, she never told them when she went off to be married. She threw a few belongings out of her bedroom window to my father each time he brought her home from a date, and then, on the day she left for ever, she climbed stealthily out of her bedroom window and let herself down to the ground, clutching her violin case.

When they married my mother's brief career came to a halt. She told us that she'd given it all up happily to be a mother. Maybe motherhood was actually a welcome escape from the cut-throat world of the performer which she had borne since childhood. Maybe she knew that there was room for only one star in their marriage, and it could not be her. Whatever the reason, she set herself to bringing up three daughters and to being a helpmeet to her husband. My father, casually taking ownership of her identity, called her 'my little Bohunk', and we moved to the depths of the English countryside so he could write in peace. We had no car, few neighbours, and of course, in those days, no television. Our home was our world.

Money was scarce throughout my childhood. The local tradesmen called regularly at the door, hoping for a little something 'on account', and my mother struggled to feed us wholesome food for pennies. Conventional housekeeping was as alien to her as Bach's *Unaccompanied Partitas* were to most housewives, but she approached it with the energy she had once expended on the violin. Every time she cooked she went into battle, and by the end the kitchen looked like the aftermath of the Somme.

But she was inventive. Stale bread was soaked in cold water and then crisped in the oven to freshen it. Stuffed ox heart, and lights smothered in garlic and paprika were our mainstays, along with sausage meat. The butcher thought we were buying the lights for the dog, but he only got the leftovers. He must have been the only dog in the area with garlic breath. Nothing was wasted. We had no refrigerator and when the milk went sour, as it often did, my mother showed us how her Transylvanian grandmother had turned sour milk into cream cheese.

Every now and then she became so homesick for Hungarian food that she tried to conjure up meals from memory on her tiny budget. She stuffed cabbage leaves with minced beef and caraway seeds, and on the rare occasions when we could afford a chicken, we had *chicken paprikas*. She made what we disparagingly called 'prunes in dough,' in an effort to recreate *szilvás gomboc*, a form of plum dumpling. She startled Bill the butcher by asking for pigs' trotters, which she boiled down to nothing, and then picked out all the bits of meat to set in aspic. Sprinkled liberally with paprika and decorated with a slice of lemon and a sprig of fresh parsley, these were served to dinner guests in small coffee cups because we had no ramekins. My father was proud of his 'little Bohunk' on these occasions, and the guests found her delightful and exotic. 'What a charming accent she has,' I overheard one say to another, 'so very foreign.' I was outraged. Accent? I heard no accent. In retrospect, I can only imagine her longing for home when she had these cooking frenzies, but we usually reacted with a cruelty specific to children, wrinkling our noses in disgust at her wilder efforts, and whining in protest.

My mother was often full of sorrow. When things were really bad she clicked open her violin case with a snap, unwrapped her violin from the silk scarf that 'kept it warm,' tightened her bow, rubbed the rosin briskly up and down the hairs, and began to tune. And as she tuned, we disappeared. Oblivious to the world around her, she frowned with passionate concentration, her fingers running up and down the strings, repeating a phrase again and again. When I heard her play with such frenzy my heart would freeze with fear, but I didn't know why. When she wasn't playing the violin she was often like a fire damped down with wet leaves—nothing much seemed to be going on, but thick smoke curled everywhere and made my eyes smart. She managed her smoke well, the signals coming over loud and clear. She was ruthless in her emotional vulnerability. Conversely, when she was happy, when the flames burned freely and the smoke dispersed, I felt almost light headed with a relief that I didn't really understand.

When debts mounted up, she taught music at a school twenty miles away. When she returned in the evening her face was grey with fatigue from a day spent listening to untalented children scratching violin strings or thumping the piano. With no bank account of her own, she handed her earnings over to my father to pay whoever was pressing the most fiercely with his bill.

We were home-schooled, so when she wasn't teaching music, she was teaching us, but when we were free of lessons, we disappeared down the garden and far into the woods out of earshot. If we were near enough to the house for our mother to hear us playing, she invariably called one of us to come and do some chore. Having had a rigidly disciplined childhood herself, she found the concept of a long and carefree afternoon just 'mucking about' quite alien. Freedom had to be earned and we had seldom earned quite enough.

Sometimes there was happy laughter—as on the day we went to hear the Vègh Quartet play at a concert nearby. Sandor Vègh had been a fellow student at the Academy in Budapest, and had created a successful and prestigious Quartet which was on a world tour. They caught sight of her in the audience, and spent the rest of the concert discreetly bowing and winking as they leaned forward to turn over a page of music. The reunion afterwards was emotional, in voluble Hungarian, and my mother looked eighteen again.

When my mother played sonatas with our neighbour Vera—a brilliant amateur pianist, we would creep through the garden to crouch under the window, drawn by the ringing sound of wonderful music. Vera, her fingers flying over the keys, plucking madly at the pizzicato bits, would call out 'Mercy! Mercy!', and when they reached the end with a deafening crescendo, they both fell about, panting with happy laughter. It was strange to hear my mother laughing so loudly and joyfully as we crouched out of sight. We children never seemed to cause such joy. Instead, each morning after breakfast came the agony of piano practice. My heart soared when I heard lovely music, and I played *con brio* in my head, but when I put my fingers to the keys I knew that as she brushed her teeth upstairs my mother was wincing in agony over every note. Occasionally I forgot myself, and let my fingers fly, my heart filled to bursting with the sheer exuberance of the music. Then I'd hear an anguished cry over the banisters: 'B *flat, not* B natural! *Please* play B flat there! And for God's sake don't BANG!' My fingers froze and my heart shrivelled with shame and fury.

As a child prodigy, my mother had found it a heavy burden to be a star. As a very ordinary child, I found it a heavy burden to be the daughter of a star. When I was little, a family friend once told me that she thought of my mother as a sleeping tiger—soft on the surface, with a fierce flame raging underneath. I don't think my father recognized that fierce flame. Why would he? He was absorbed in his writing, and she was just his 'little Bohunk.' We never recognized it either, just as we never questioned the smoke of her melancholy and the ferocious energy with which she played the violin. Why would we? She was just our mother.

In Her Hands

Pat Clifford

*Praise the world to the angel; leave the unsayable aside ...
... show him what is ordinary, what has been
shaped from generation to generation, shaped by hand
    and eye.
Tell him of things. He will stand still in astonishment
the way you stood by the rope maker in Rome
or beside the potter on the Nile.*
Rilke "The Ninth Elegy"

Regina in the 50s and the background wash of memories from an ordinary prairie childhood: gumbo and blizzards; buttery summer sunshine and adults oddly confused about whether it was cold enough/hot enough/dry enough/wet enough for you, eh?

Swarms of kids in wartime housing, raiding gardens, playing soldiers across half a dozen lawns. We'd hunker down under the front bedroom window dodging the rat-a-tat-tat of my mother's typing from behind enemy lines. I sang "Kiss Me Goodnight Sergeant Major" when the other kids only knew stupid grown up songs like the Pepsodent toothpaste jingle from the radio.

Dads with injuries: missing legs, shot-out front teeth, bum backs.

The English Girls, which is what my mother and her war bride friends called themselves for decades. Christmas food hampers sent "home" for at least 10 years after the war ended. Bluebirds and white cliffs of Dover as real in my head as meadow larks and the parched hills of the Qu'Appelle Valley where we took day trips on rickety wooden trains with hard bench seats and windows you could open from the top or from the bottom, and stick your arm out but watch out just in case it might accidentally get cut off, for chrissake.

My mother was one of almost 50,000 war brides—the largest mass immigration in Canadian history, and surely one of its oddest, comprising only women and children. For decades after the war, no one thought much about them. They were just the mums who embarrassed you by saying tomato wrong, just the neighbours with suspicious habits like reading in the afternoon or paying good money to send out the laundry every Friday. They were only the wives who had snapped up all the marriageable men or the odd duck daughters-in-law who didn't know a damn thing worth knowing, honestly.

When she got off the train to meet her Canadian family, my mother had no domestic talents at all, had never heard of bridge or canasta or fowl suppers, could not swap recipes or remedies for croup. She'd never gutted a chicken or hung wet sheets on a line at twenty below. Following the instructions of a Scottish child-rearing book she boiled diapers till the steam in our slummy Germantown shack peeled all the veneer off the furniture. She had to be shown how to can gleaming jars of peaches in the hot August sun.

But my mother also owned a Remington typewriter, not one she brought from Scotland with her, although I would have loved the romance of it if she had. I don't know if she and my father had stretched his weekly pay packet enough to buy her this one real thing, this one tangible connection between the life she had led when she started work at 14 as a clerk typist, the way a rich man might have bought his wife a dress coat with a fox collar and boots just for good. Perhaps they got it because she needed it in some way for the job she was forced to take when my father got injured at work—maybe to bring her skills back up to scratch, or to do piece work from home.

However it came into my life, that typewriter was a beauty, like the ones that sometimes fill the screen at the start of old private eye movies where cryptic messages move across a hard rubber roller, magnified, fuzzy letter by magnified letter hammered into soft paper. Or the way some novelist pounds out The End and rips out the last page with a dramatic, grinding whirl of the platen that my mother would never, ever have permitted.

I loved everything about it. Heavy as a boat anchor I might have said long before I actually knew what a boat anchor was, there was also a graceful transparency in its own writing, and that my mother never did learn to master. My finger pads still remember round keys with raised chrome edges, one for each letter, number and piece of punctuation you could use to write a poem or pay a bill or send bad news across the Atlantic. And the elegant fan of the type bars, those long silvery rods that connected the round keys with the upside down print face.

First learning to read, I was puzzled by these keys arranged not in the ABC order of the alphabet song I could sing all the way to the end of the street and back. The QWERTY keyboard is an odd vestigial organ, like an appendix, designed precisely as proof against young stenographers like my mother whose fingers were trained to fly at 60, 70, even 80 words a minute. The nonsensical configuration was meant to slow them down so that the type bars would not jam the way they did whenever I tried to make them work.

I cannot imagine what speed my mother could have accomplished had these strangers not decided in advance that skills such as hers were too much for their own invention. And I am surprised by the intensity of my certainty that they were somehow in anonymous cahoots with the aunts and neighbours who, if they looked at my mother's typewriter at all, somehow held it against her, somehow condemned in advance its foreignness to the lives they knew. Little did they know. Little did I know.

Typewriters had ribbons then, either plain black or striped in half, black at the top and red at the bottom. You threaded the ribbon through carefully from right to left, slipping it through the wire teeth of a rectangular metal mouth through which each key hammered. Sometimes the ribbon popped out the way a bra strap comes unhitched, and then the ribbon rucked up and you had to dig in and stretch it out, an inevitably messy business that often left smudges on the paper and the need to start over if the document you were working on was important enough to warrant spinning the paper off the roller and cranking a new sheet into its place.

Erasing was a nightmare. One false keystroke (or you hoped only one before you noticed), and you had to stop everything. Using the big chrome carriage return, the one that reminds me of large faucets in handicapped washrooms you can turn on and off with your elbow in case there's germs, you positioned the paper at one end or the other of the roller so that crumbs didn't fall into the works and gum them up. Then rubbing carefully with the hard edge of a round eraser, you tried to take out the error without tearing a ragged hole or leaving black streaks because the rubber had somehow got greasy. A quick flick of the little brush attached to the eraser and two sharp puffs blown against the paper and you were ready to carefully, oh so carefully, reposition the carriage so that the proper letter now jumped through the hole at exactly the right spot, neither high nor low, covering the offending mistake.

You took all this bother only if you weren't typing legal documents, where no erasure, no matter how perfect, was permitted. "Even the last word on the last line," my mother used to tell me in the same singsong voice she used for stories, "if you got that wrong you had to start the whole page over." She spoke as if she knew only too well. And I wondered how you could keep from getting impossibly scared and clumsy knowing everything had been perfect right up to the last instant. I knew my own small fingers and large fears would have betrayed me time and again, and I loved to hear how she learned hardly ever to do things wrong.

And the sounds. Not my fingernail clacks on a keyboard, but solid strikes, perfectly rhythmical claps if you were good the way my mother was good. Each line, copied rapidly or composed at exactly the speed that thoughts formed themselves through bone and tendon, was marked by the ping of a bell that commanded a smart snap of the carriage return and the start of a new line. I loved hearing my mother's hands make those sounds, but years later when I was learning to type in school, I also discovered how vulnerable you are, sitting in a room full of others whose machines sound off more often, more reliably, more gracefully than your own. Anyone walking behind you, or even a bored substitute teacher dozing off at the front of the room can tell without effort who is genuinely up to speed and whose fingers need to be rapped with a ruler.

So much to remember in this one ordinary thing: watching my mother insert the blue onion skin of air mail paper on which she typed letters to her own mother whom she did not get to see for years after the war, knowing which paper face would turn out be front and which would be back when it was folded up and all the flaps licked and sealed, ready for the mailbox that was their only connection; the gorgeous, extravagant gold letters that spelled Remington across the face of the machine; the stiff plastic cover that she draped over everything when she was done and it was time to pick up some household chore she had more recently learned to master.

So much that now lives only in the war stories she told me, not when I was a child, but only much later. When I was little, war stories were what the dads told if they spoke about those times at all. So I didn't know until I was an adult that she had used just such a typewriter when she was conscripted into the British army and was posted to the south of England. Assigned a rickety table set in the loft of a commandeered apple barn, my mother, whose appalling eyesight was overlooked in the cursory medical exam, worked for weeks on sheets of paper written in some kind of code—mostly numbers, certainly nothing that made the kind of sense that allows you to touch type with fingerprint accuracy, knowing as soon as you have done it that you have hit a wrong key.

Peering through the weak afternoon light peppered with dust motes and struggling with cold fingers against the inadequate heat thrown by a cantankerous corner stove she had to light each morning, my mother had struggled for perfect accuracy.

The work was top secret. She was required to take each page, sheet by sheet as it fell from the roller of her machine, and place it directly in the hands of her commanding officer.

So secret that all she knew was that there were women in other equally secret places elsewhere in England typing other words and figures that would have to be combined to make the pages complete.

So secret that, until she was taken to military encampments on the beaches and nearby woods right before the invasion of Normandy, she did not know that the orders for D Day had passed through her fingers. Operation Overlord was about to begin, and she stood beside her commanding officer in a marshalling area that held 6,000 soldiers ready to follow her typed orders, ready to invade France. It was, she said, completely and horribly silent.

Now, at ninety, my mother carries this tiny bit of history in her palsied hands.

Hoop

Jeanette Lynes

When we considered
the modern inventions
we wondered what all
the fuss was about—
saran wrap?—nothing
wrong with waxed paper!
Power steering came for cars,
not tractors—we bumped
over the stubble as ever before.
Super glue failed to fasten
money in wallets—the decisive *thwuck*
of my mother's purse clicking shut
did the trick just as well.
We heard about a pill
to stop babies. *Tell me*
another one, my mother said.
The only true, good idea
all those years, the hula hoop.
It spun especially well
positioned high on women
eight months gone.
The woman had only to gyrate
slow and imperceptible
as the planet itself.
Then when she felt ready
to deliver, cast off the hoop,
climb onto the tractor.

MARY (FOLEY) DOYLE

Marjorie Doyle

Born 1917 in Point Mall, Placentia Bay, Newfoundland.
Died 2006 in St. John's, Newfoundland, aged 88.

Mary was raised in Corner Brook, far from her parents' native Placentia Bay. Work had lured them west. Her mother was a determined redhead whose genius was to feed and clothe seven daughters and a son on a mill worker's wage.

Mary graduated from St. Henry's, narrowly missed a university scholarship, and took "Commercial." She dipped briefly into the steno pool of Bowater's, but soon became private secretary to the mill's traffic manager. One day, offered the rare opportunity to make a long distance call, she phoned a Water Street merchant in remote St. John's, replying to an ad. Impressed, he hired her.

Three years later, Mary married the boss, Gerald Doyle. He was now a widower, 25 years older than her, and living on an eight-acre estate. She stepped into a household with maids, a cook and a gardener—and five young motherless boys. Dinner parties, New York business trips, cruises and summers sailing around Newfoundland—she'd been swept into a world of glamour, travel, and love. When he died in 1956, he left a bewildered 39-year-old with three more small children in the mix.

She was thrown immediately into a man's world. As "Chairman" of her husband's Manufacturer's Agency, she was in charge of 50 employees. The key to the business was a close relationship with the principals of Canadian companies like Kimberly Clark, Boyle Midway, Warner Lambert. She set out for central Canada to assure them she could carry on the business. She won them over, and returned home to oversee the growing firm.

Mary Doyle never felt at home with St. John's "society." She sought company, and found it in the Redemptorist priests—intelligent, urbane men who posed no threat to her widowhood. They shared her moral perspectives and respected her. In her home, they smoked cigars, listened to opera, and talked books.

The mother of our childhood was stunning, decisive, and slightly scary. She wore a sealskin jacket, drove a Land Rover and had two German Shepherds. If a man hesitated when approaching her, she'd exclaim: A man who's afraid of dogs! She was fearless, bought and sold property without advice, and travelled without reservations— including a three month European tour with kids. Later, she drove around Morocco in an Austin mini. Fearless, yet she once opened the front door, and ordered a passing teenager to come in and catch a mouse cowering behind the piano.

At 53, her family raised, Mary walked into a classroom of 17-year-olds and began university. She took notes in shorthand, asked smart questions, and wrote A papers. At 57 she crossed the stage to collect a first class history degree. The photo records a proud and defiant woman.

Mary was anti-Confederate. Returning Canadian? she'd be asked at a border. I carry a Canadian passport. Canadian citizen? I was born in Point Mall. Eventually, a frustrated guard would let her pass. Her rage against Canada dates from 1939 when an Immigration officer on a Halifax dock looked down at her seven-year-old Down Syndrome sister. He removed the child to a holding cell and next day handed her back: *Entry Denied.*

Mary was a fighter. Stacks of yellow paper document responses to injustice. In 1969 she fumed in a church pew on Fogo Island while a priest "harangued his own good people." She wrote him about what he had "flung with vituperation" to "a captive audience who could not speak back." She copied the bishop.

Her independence strengthened as she aged. At 77 she was tough enough to cope with the blow of losing a leg. For months her car sat idle in the driveway; she couldn't relinquish this symbol of mobility. In time, she installed a lift that she rode to a waiting wheelchair downstairs. She'd open the garage door remotely and take a cab to the bank. She—and her dog—carried on through the Newfoundland winters for five years. She moved in briefly with her youngest son then, with courage and insight, made the inevitable move to a home. She was a rebel, and fires of defiance continued to burn even as her world grew smaller. She hung a bold sign on the door: *No admittance after 11:00 p.m.* She didn't want staff checking on her. On Fridays, she'd wheel down the corridor for linens, then back to work her way around the bed, tucking in the fresh sheets. It took an hour, but she would not give up.

Mary was a devout Catholic. She accepted death without fear, and passed peacefully.

Reading Shakespeare

E. Alex Pierce

She looks under the pillow. She cannot find her words. She keeps
a little list. How did she write that out? A list of pencilled cursives
sketched on scraps of foolscap paper, irregular verbs—something
she'd give her high-school students. How *lie* becomes *lay, write*
becomes *wrote—smite, smote.* "I lay in the bed all day. I would like
to write you, but my pen would not obey me, so—" She stops.

He says, *Devouring time.* He says, *Let us not*
to the marriage. Says—*thou art more lovely.* She sighs.
The list goes back under the pillow.

She cannot not remember. She cannot read the words,
small *and's* and *the's* and *now's* and *after's*—linkages
she cannot make. *Out damned spot*—there is no perfume
to sweeten or to make forget. Sometimes, after reading,
I put my head down on her chest, and rest there
on the flannel nightgown. There is no end to this.

THE SAME ROOF

Denise Chong

Hardly had Winnie brought the new baby, another daughter, home from the hospital when they had the inconvenience of having to move again. The landlord living downstairs was annoyed when Winnie replaced the twenty-five-watt bulb in the hall with a sixty-watt without asking him first.

Chan Sam had his own ideas about what his daughter's next move should be. "Everybody is buying a house," he said. He persuaded them to look at what he'd found for sale, a modest two-bedroom house on Gladstone Street off the Kingsway, close to the Canada Dry Factory. Winnie and John liked the neighbourhood. There was a United Church across the street and on one side was a gray stucco house with a white picket fence, and on the other, a purple stucco house. Both were immaculately kept. The house itself had an above-ground basement; the siding was of fashionable grey-green asphalt tiles; there was a gas fireplace in the living room, a sun porch, a well-tended lawn in the front and a garden in the back. It was being sold furnished. The asking price was $7,800. The problem was raising the $1,100 down payment. John's eldest sister was happy to lend him the money, and Chan Sam insisted he wanted to contribute. "Put a little more down," he said, "and then the monthly payment is just like paying rent." Winnie accepted his $900 graciously, knowing nothing would please her father more than to be able to boast in Chinatown: "I bought my daughter a house."

In return for his contribution, her father moved into the second bedroom. Winnie, John, their two-year-old and the baby, less than one year, shared the other bedroom. The closeness bothered no one. One of the jobs the employment agency in Chinatown found Chan Sam was cleaning a hotel three mornings a week. No matter how late she'd been up the night before, Winnie rose at four to cook him rice before he started work at five. Her father in turn sometimes babysat when she had to help at the cleaners. He still spent most of his free time in Chinatown, taking the bus there, stopping in at his clan society to pick up his mail. He never came back empty-handed; he always brought something back for dinner—some greens, maybe a fresh rock cod. John was happy enough to propose a weekend trip together. Chan Sam had often said he'd always wanted to visit the United States. Except for being hassled on both sides of the border by officials suspicious that anyone Chinese might be a Communist and therefore have links to an enemy power, the trip to Seattle was pleasant enough, especially for Chan Sam, who was wide-eyed at the eight-lane freeways on the American side.

Winnie never insulted her father by asking, but it seemed to her that although he worked only periodically and drew a modest pension, he always had a few dollars to spare. There was the money he'd given them for the house, for example. She thought he must also be sending a few dollars here and there home to China, because he'd said to her: "Ah, Hing, if things get better for you and I am gone from the world, all I ask is that you keep up sending money to China—twenty or so dollars every couple of months." Even though Winnie said she'd have to ask John, she knew she couldn't ask her husband to carry that obligation. He had been resolutely against taking in her little brother, Leonard; how could he agree to support a family she herself had never met?

I was Winnie and John's second-born, and one of my earliest memories is of my grandfather, whom I knew as *Goong-goong* (the proper way to address a maternal grandfather), bringing me a red tricycle, the first present I remember receiving from anyone. I can also picture him coming through the back door of our Gladstone Street house, setting down a shopping bag of groceries and scooping me up. I remember too my sister and I sitting in pails of water in the backyard cooling off on warm summer days, reassured by his presence as he worked nearby in the garden.

It was on a day like that that he and my mother got into one of those silly disputes that blew up into something unintended. Mother was down in the basement, standing at the wringer washer. She was diverting the hot soapy water from the wash cycle into pails, intending to reuse the water to wash the floors upstairs. My grandfather came down with the garden tools, put them in the sink and turned on the hot water to rinse them off.

"*Baba,* why don't you use the cold water to rinse off the garden tools?" she asked. He was immediately offended. "I'm going to write to the family in China to tell them this is how you treat your own father!" he said. He went into a sulk, and Mother couldn't understand why.

Finally, he broke the silence. "If that's the way you're going to be, I don't think we can live under the same roof," he said.

Mother did not talk back, for only then did she realize how unhappy her father was living away from Chinatown. He'd been away three years. At the Gladstone Street house, only she spoke enough Chinese to converse with him. For company during the day, there were only the neighbours, old Mr. Penny, a night watchman, and his wife, tending their flowers behind their white picket fence, or else Mr. and Mrs. Stewart, a retired couple who rarely ventured out. Mother knew her father could hardly admit he no longer wanted to live in his daughter's house, not when it had been his idea to buy it. He moved back to Chinatown, to the Sun Ah Hotel where he'd lived before, and he rather enjoyed taking the bus when he came to visit us. I always went running to the door, my arms outstretched to meet his.

THE MAD AND
BEAUTIFUL MOTHERS

Denied Peace of Mind
by
"Calendar Fear?"

Have you ever wondered how other women can go happily about their daily tasks, while you are tormented by the haunting spectre of "Calendar Fear"? The worry and apprehension that come from "Calendar Fear" are now so unnecessary.

Thousands of women like yourself have discovered the easy way to avoid "Calendar Fear" forever. That way is the **"Lysol"** way ... the *proved* method of regular feminine hygiene.

You see, **"Lysol"** kills germ-life instantly — on contact. Yet **"Lysol"** is perfectly harmless to delicate feminine tissues. **"Lysol"** has enjoyed the confidence of the medical profession for over 50 years ... and because it is diluted with water before use, **"Lysol"** costs less than one cent a treatment!

BANISH CALENDAR FEAR WITH

"Lysol"
Brand Disinfectant

For more information, clip and mail this coupon now

THE MAD AND BEAUTIFUL MOTHERS

Patricia Young

We are the children of the fifties
with the mad and beautiful mothers.
In the forties they went to movies in toeless
high-heels, smoked cigarettes, and dreamed
of Leslie Howard, their madness
occurring some time later.

Perhaps it struck the night we were born
or that day at the park, swinging from our knees
we slipped from the bars. After that,
clotheslines collapsed in every back yard,
and children fell through the air
like bombs in September.

We left for school and they barricaded the doors
with living room furniture. Later,
we climbed in through basement windows,
twisted and jived to rock'n roll
while upstairs our mothers bent over sinks,
unable to wash their hair.

We hid our mothers from our friends,
our friends from our mothers. Thunder
and lightning and some disappeared into closets
or hospitals from which they never emerged.
Perhaps madness first struck on that flight
from Amsterdam, London, Glasgow, the cabin
hot and crowded, and rain seeping in.

We learned to shift our lives
around and through them where they sat
at the dining room table staring through doors
in the wallpaper for days at a time.

We are the children who survived the fifties
and their mothers, even their conversations with God.

It has taken us years to forgive them
their madness, though they loved us despite it.
Years to go back to the muggy afternoons
the whole world reeked of spice and sweat and vinegar.

It is late August and our mothers are in the kitchen
pickling beets and cucumbers.
Like fiends they are pickling
silver-skinned onions
and anything else
that gets in their way.

Rescuing Mickey

Sarah Murphy

Every time i see a photo of that plane half submerged in the water surrounded by ferries miracle on the hudson they're calling it now i find myself reminded of my mother and it's not just the mickey murphy award for waterfront journalism named after her something someone reporting on that incident could have won it's the water taxi that does it what a perfect image mickey murphy the water taxi all jaunty like our fifties favourite tommy the tugboat a bug-eyed face grinning from her bridge maybe a little cabby's cap above her new york cab yellow water taxi body an unfiltered chesterfield stuck in her crooked mouth for an era that still celebrated smoking moving back and forth from brooklyn to manhattan pier eleven to the red hook ikea picking up all sorts of guys tourists businessmen lawyers drug dealers numbers runners with her favourites no doubt the sailors two men at least always on board maybe not a great children's book but *mickey murphy the water taxi* the perfect book for adult children of alcoholics the way instead of toot toot her horn would roar *outatheway buncha phonies buncha phonies* at any watercraft in her way you can see why i imagine her one of fourteen of new york water taxi vessels called out to the site of that crash what a way to spend extra purgatorial time on earth to make up for her misdeeds the mickey murphy to the rescue even if

there never was any rescuing mickey ...

While you could be sure that horn would roar its loudest not at tankers harbour tugs garbage scows but at the new seadoos the yachts taking over the harbour just as mickey shouted best did her little dance not at montero's the seaman's bar where tim and i were mostly raised or at the wigwam the bar of the mainly mohawk construction workers but in manhattan at tim costello's the bar of the new yorker literary crowd *buncha phonies buncha phonies* blaming its denizens for her first husband mark murphy's writer's block and for his death holed up drinking his way to oblivion in his johannesburg hotel room during the passbook riots of 1952 while they in turn blamed her how she aimed the biggest sharpest insults at mark calling his self doubt weak maudlin balless irish catholic self-pity she came from solid middle class middle west protestant stock even if she loved the ethnic and gender confusion of being called mick to his murph ridiculing too his effeminate lack of combat experience writing for air force magazine in the war until the only literati who would stick by her were bob and vicky gerdie and joe mitchell who always took us to dinner in chinatown and told us how mark had invented the classic new yorker profile though mickey would talk of shawn and jim agee at the funeral too and deploy mark at every opportunity as some kind of unrealized genius to establish her place and ours in that literary world recreate us as baby journalists estrange us from the world around us the tough working class bar life she had chosen then turned the anniversary of both his birth and death july thirty-first the day he was to turn forty into her own private *buncha phonies* memorial the days for the most outrageous antics when the more you tried to help the worse she would get like on the subways when she wouldn't get off no matter what we did and with each attempt louder crazier urinating or attacking strangers even later in my twenties in mexico bent out of shape and suicidal and when i get friends to drive me down from mexico city to cuernavaca the first thing she does is insult them then strip naked and crawl into the bath i don't think i was ever around her another july thirty-first it had long been obvious enough

there never was any rescuing mickey ...

Got herself fired from time life that *buncha phonies* way too twice in fact first right after mark's death then didn't hold a steady job for more than a decade said she was freelance but never finished anything kept declaring she didn't have writers' block she wasn't a writer mark was the writer she was a reporter a researcher bought the line that practicality not creativity was woman's lot accepted the fairness of the way time life wouldn't hire women as writers until the law made them long after she'd been fired the second time for insulting her editor stayed quiet a record three years just long enough for me to win a time life sponsored national merit scholarship that was a practical move too get yourself the right man she said threw my drawings straight out the door during my art school years what was i trying for anyway phoney that i was there never were never would be any great women artists my favourite project of mickey's was the early fifties book on what to do with children in new york what to do to children in new york i would call it later though it was good for us bought us some relief got us out to some free places and into some we could never afford she got a whopping big advance for that one too people still wanted to rescue her help out the poor widow i remember the reams of yellow paper coming off the black typewriter how she kept talking between visits to day camps and amusement parks and museums and swimming pools and bottles of cutty sark of how this time she had it nailed she knew how to put it together then more reams of paper off the typewriter the book still unfinished and then there's finding all that yellow paper all the damn drafts in her archives after she died all of mark's stuff nestled alongside i read them both mick and murph together over and over and hers was just as good i'm telling you just as good lively insightful stiff upper lip perky objective fifties journalism with a real voice sitting there on the page she never did pay that advance back she was blacklisted for years

there never was any rescuing mickey ...

Even if she did make a romantic rescue out of the encounter with my dad down at montero's said it was the night of the day she'd broken her last heel on her last pair of dress shoes to go into manhattan to look for a job went down to the bar to cash a check joe and pilar were the last in the neighbourhood she could count on they'd cash her checks even when they knew she wasn't good for the money and there he was cherokee bill the choctaw sailor they'd had an affair years before of which apparently i was the result he hadn't docked on the east coast for years so eyes locking and love at first re-sight and us waking to him in her bed the next day only just like with everyone else as the years went by the more he tried the more she acted out insults to the only good dead indian of his prick and taunting him with the most down and out men she could pick up while when he wasn't at sea he was cooking and cleaning and managing the house too it was mickey's pride she'd never baked a brownie put on an apron or worked a woman's page no lack of food or money to buy it ever enough to make her apply for a working class job either despite the multi-racial mix of working class men she kept about to tell stories in the kitchen then once or twice a year she'd try a dinner party the way she had way back when for the literati cooking in the ground floor kitchen hauling the food up into the butler's pantry in the dumbwaiter rushing up the stairs to the second floor to haul it out to the dining room to put it on the table in that old house built for a small family and two servants only she seldom got out of the kitchen after a while totally sloshed by the time the guests arrived causing one to say mickey is a great cook if you arrive in time to rescue the food so food yes mickey no

there never was any rescuing mickey ...

Then one day before you know it the fifties will have given way to the sixties and the sixties to the seventies then the eighties the nineties until one afternoon well past the millennium there i'll be partying with tim and a bunch of travel agents on the maiden voyage of the mickey murphy people asking mickey murphy who was he as i walk across the upper deck beer in hand breathing salt air outside on a perfect new york day edward hopper light on the stone towers of the brooklyn bridge the red brick projects of the lower east side the warehouses of red hook while i wonder what kind of mickey murphy tale to tell them thinking back on what's in that naming the moment only months before at her memorial on a barge under the brooklyn bridge over two hundred people present and the representative of brooklyn's borough president regaling us with stories of mickey poking him and any number of men like him big and conscious of their power six feet tall and counting in the chest backing them into corners saying *listen kiddo* as she advocated for the people of low income fort greene in the development of the

brooklyn waterfront concerned still that there always be something
for all children to do in new york flashy with her white hair and her
purple scarves and suits yes she was an old woman who did wear
purple shorter than ever in advanced osteoporosis but with her
voice still gravelly and as easy to mistake for a man's *listen kiddo*
poke poke certainly much better than *buncha phonies* jiggle jiggle
with him adding to appreciative laughter *we weren't all her kids but
we were all her kiddos* to make me wonder what made that change
certainly it was no twelve step program there never was any letting
go and letting god any taking of responsibility or even recognition
of what she had done bad night after bad night the morning after
bringing only the drinking of milk and real or pretended memory
loss never even a scathing let it all hang out memoir maybe phoney
for her *buncha phonies* something better to read than to live while
all i know is that just as it takes more than one ferry to rescue a
shitload of passengers from a sinking aircraft's wings it might take
that whole river of changes that sank the fifties to rescue one person
so that as the years went by mickey acted more and acted out less
owed maybe to so many more ways to be a woman or a man the
recognition of the political in the personal the subjective in the
objective the thinning of the boundaries of race and class or maybe
to the irony of gentrification that she could live well off the rent
from the upper stories of her house no worries about our next meal
or her last unmet deadline so maybe that's the way to go tell about
the pioneering woman journalist and waterfront activist only as i
turn to a travel agent to say mickey murphy was my mother the little
ferry that can chooses to do a little arrhythmic dance to cavitate a
little with a buck and a twist and there i am flat on my ass soaked
in beer with tim giving me a hand up saying trust mickey for the
knock out punch when you least expect it so yes i can imagine a
crooked little grin on a yellow tippling tommy tugboat face but i'm
suddenly seasick nauseous again and the nausea won't subside not
then not now no matter how humorous or objective i think i can be
i was never a baby journalist never even her kiddo i was just her kid
so maybe it's time to quit forget about it say nothing and enjoy the
view admit it never was my job for me

there never will be any rescuing mickey ...

EULOGY FOR EUNICE

Mary Jane Copps

My mother, Mary Margaret Eunice Connolly, was trapped between history and genetics. She died at the age of 50, when I was 15. And although it wasn't obvious, or even swift, she died at her own hand, complications from drinking Drano months before.

⌯

Eunice was born into squatter's poverty in 1923. My grandfather's support of workers' rights blackballed him from the mines and logging mills that created most of the wages in small towns like Kirkland Lake, Ontario. There was never enough money to feed, clothe and house my grandmother and their eight surviving children.

But Eunice blossomed in spite of this harshness. She was an exotic creature—beautiful, charming, intelligent. And while she always understood the power of beauty and charm, she was most proud of her intelligence.

Her goal was to build a much different life for herself, to excel at school, to go to university. But her father had different plans—and he was firm. Everyone, every child, had to contribute to the household, bring in a wage as soon as possible. Eunice was told to follow the commercial program. There was no discussion.

She was shattered, enraged by this decision. In the years I was audience to her alcohol-soaked orations, this was always the opening chorus—anger at her father for not allowing her to go to university.

But history intervened. The war called out for skilled people and Eunice had skills. She typed over 120 words a minute, had the speediest of shorthand, never erred on an adding machine. The Women's Royal Naval Service welcomed her and sent her to Washington where, as when she was a schoolgirl, she drew people to her, a bevy of girlfriends who pinned each other's hair each night and swooned over Frank Sinatra on the radio. The war and urban living showed Eunice a life of exciting work, high praise, music, dancing, and not one thought of poverty or hunger.

And of course, there were boys, men who vied for her attention by the dozens. There is a black and white photo I cherish of four naval officers walking near the White House. The women, stunning in their jaunty hats and fitted uniforms, are between two tall young marines. My mother looks straight ahead, smiling into the camera. Everyone else is smiling too, but their eyes are on her.

When the war ended Eunice was given the chance to go to university, a government's thanks for her service. And jobs were waiting for her—commanding officers she'd worked with in Washington had businesses in downtown Toronto and they wrote letters asking her to join their firms. But she returned home first, to help out the family, take time to make the right decision.

Her brothers were home from the war as well, one of them friends with an air force veteran, a handsome young redhead from nearby Timmins. An invitation was sent and Leo Michael Copps took the train to Kirkland Lake to visit and attend a weekend dance.

It happened in a moment—just like in the movies, the novels, the songs. Lee held Eunice in his arms and all the other boys faded away. Love arrived and the future was shaped by the words between kisses.

Lee had studied interior design with his government money, and started his own business. In their twice-daily letters to each other, they talked about how Eunice would help at the new store and of when they would move the business to Toronto.

But money was tight, the hours long and Lee waffled constantly on a wedding date. Eunice wanted a firm decision regardless of money, she said, or she'd go to Toronto without him.

The ultimatum worked and, in every photo of their simple winter wedding, they beam in anticipation of a beautiful future. Soon afterwards, turned down by the bank, Lee borrowed money from his mother to support the growing business and in return he agreed to keep the store in Timmins awhile longer. This broken promise became the second chorus of drunken, angry speeches.

Their lives followed a well-documented, post-war pattern. Eunice worked in the store until she got pregnant, had three children in six years, consulted her well-worn Dr. Spock. But another pattern emerged too, a genetic one. Eunice, like the majority of her siblings, suffered from mental illness: dark moods, extreme highs, uncontrollable rage. She embraced alcohol as a mood stabilizer, drank steadily throughout each day.

She did seek help. Doctors were generous in their provision of uppers and downers designed specifically for female complaints. Narcotics were prescribed too, for a back injury suffered when she delivered my oldest brother.

So the trap was firmly set: Eunice was drugged and drunk and crazy in a world where no one talked about anything other than recipes and floor wax.

⟨⟨⟩⟩

At the time of her death, my mother and I had come full circle, through frighteningly angry and sometimes violent times, to the calm and gentle friendship of my childhood. She became the younger, in need of my patience and attention, and I, trying on adulthood, was the one who held her hand.

Our last moments together were rushed. It was the closing night of my high school's production of *The Music Man*, and I needed to get to the auditorium. But I found her in the bathroom closet, shivering in her yellow cotton nightgown, moving a half-full bottle of rubbing alcohol toward her lips.

Gently, I turned her around, walked her back to the bedroom. I covered her in blankets until the chills began to subside. I know now that these were the hardest moments, the ones between bender and sobriety. Anything could happen in her mind, to her body, and she was terrified.

I sat with her, held her hand and talked, listed all the reasons she needed to stop drinking, including recovering from the surgery that had repaired the ravages of the Drano. And she talked to me, not in loud angry tones but in those of a lost little girl. She talked of sorrow and loneliness and fear—fear of Hell and Purgatory, fear of the future, fear of sobriety. I listened, squeezed her hand, told her I loved her. I left her drifting off to sleep. She died hours later, her fragile throat collapsing around an arrowroot biscuit.

∞

I have been grieving my mother for 39 years, her tragic, too-short life becoming a mirror in which I have constantly judged myself. In the early years, the image I saw propelled me to do the opposite. I found my way to Toronto, made it my home, graduated from university. I've kept my own name and bank account, remained cautious with alcohol, never chosen a china pattern.

I've also seen what is similar, for I am very much my mother's daughter. This has kept me on a tightrope, waiting for that moment, that unguarded second, when enthusiasm, energy and anxiety turn against me, place me into the solitary confinement of mental illness.

Fortunately, that moment has never arrived. Instead, much to my surprise, I've discovered a heritage of courage and hope—a gift from Eunice I've only recently acknowledged.

At the age of 41, when I was six, she joined AA, lived with the small town jealousies and judgment of her, the only female member. Each year sober held its own nervous breakdown, the arrival of which was always humiliating and the recovery always a battle. Yet she continued to believe that things would get better, that she could be better if she kept trying, kept going to confession, kept having faith.

Until the last battle, the one where she looked in the mirror and saw what I see now. It was only when I turned 50 that I understood what happened in those last three years, why she began to drink again, why her actions were edged with suicide.

There was the weight gain. Her lovely hourglass figure began to soften and the closet that contained a wardrobe of glamour and beauty became a silent accusation of failure. There was me, the accidental fourth child with whom she'd been friends, entering puberty and asserting my independence, excluding her. There were new wrinkles around eyes and mouth, and endless grey hairs, a need to pluck not only eyebrows but chin and lip. And there was the unanticipated change in how others treated her. Suddenly the power of beauty and charm was no longer hers—and she believed it to be too late to build a life with her intelligence.

She lost all hope. There was a tragic moment when her mirror revealed that she would never go to university, that Toronto would remain a dream, that she was old in a place that she hated, living a life she never wanted.

Mom, I'm sorry that courage and hope didn't carry you through, that I didn't understand more while you were alive, that we were never mother and daughter as adults. But know that I think about you every day. And when I stand in front of my mirror, tweezers at the ready, I look into the eyes we share and I ask you to come with me, to be part of a different history, stronger genetics, kinder aging.

GOOD MOTHER

deborah schnitzer

when my mother died I was very mad at   her because at forty one
I discovered   she had not told me everything
and I thought that she had
wasn't I her confidante by the sink, at four, bruised,
her hands in dishwater, dry in winter, swollen in summer heat, rings
embedded in her married finger, hands entirely musical
soaped, nails thickening he did not like her to play she said I hate

at six I remember rooting for   her because she tried to leave
                                    he could not cope with
                                        did not really like

            her own father brought her back

she lay in bed for years
said don't marry and if you do for
money only and then when you have to
go there's cash you can wear nice things in your houses, travel

she said to me about my father
            be nice to him he   doesn't mean
            don't stir things up (as if I were a ladle)
            please she said just do what he says
                        I do
                  disappear is the first word he wakes
I hear it in the kitchen sneaking baker's chocolate hiding
in my closet gum drops jersey milk cigarettes
when I am twelve and they are sleeping pills

please she asks just do what I say
I try to mince with words late at night when
we are holding each other in the kitchen dishes
almost done and she is
anxious to

please
dream she says when I do at eighteen
                        bring him home she is appalled,
   murderous, how could you for he is
                        penniless, raw

all through the road I take before I leave the town I am
growing in if we are walking down the street past store
windows that magnify the size we have become she says
        please tell me I am a good mother
        I know I am not a good mother
        I wanted to be a good mother

I tell her she is the very good of good mothers and I think
this is true

        even when she climbs the stairs through our childhood,
        sighing blaming us for the dust we make when living
        beds unmade, socks sour,
                        toothpaste rimming the bathroomcup

        even when frantic she won't stop him beating our names
        called stupid and his face lathered pushing
                one down
                        the stair
                                another into the snow bare I think
she is a good
mother because now I know at fifty-nine
if there were pills and the better word from someone
she could see weekly who might say

if you cannot leave him then protect

do I know

she loved him

yes she might at night for they could talk, pillows,
in our new house, where we go when I am nine, we hear
through vents from the second floor what do they have
to say to one another that does not sound like you dirty rotten
if I get my hands on you what kind of bullshit is

they sound soft
we wonder who they are

she never says wait until your father because he charges
everything except Tuesday when he is at a   meeting
and we love that meeting better and better
                                        because
                    5 o'clock and there
          are grilled cheese
sandwiches, ketchup, french fries, pepsi sprawling, seconds,
maybe thirds and the walls are never splattered with plates
tossed our fingers easy on the table heart beats regular

when she says he's sick because and we come home
from university in the spring
    we know how long before the doctor and the needles
and the monitor   like the way he lost his teeth in the war
but never said we know he wears false we always know that
he wears false in front of strangers   brag and show but he does
not like the way we breathe our teeth
with cavities and monthly bills he cannot pay for us

she says he loves but she never says he is a good father because
on road trips in the fifties
     when he turns to swat
    or sting with spit the way his words fly
she says he cannot control because
                 he dies in the middle of the night
when I am forty his heart failing
    (his heart failing did he have an organ
playing in the folds of our newborn
whimper did he carry that would he
find the smell of just coming dear

           why not)

I rush home, wet, tears I have never wasted coming quick
into the kitchen I am looking for my mother free and she is damp,
inconsolable, holding dead love letters from the war which say
I love and she is sure he did not deserve her but more better

good mother gone to seed hoped for reawakening stuffed
in my throat she says great man he was, the street people
he has smiled at over years and meetings good works

surely he has done there are so many gathered in the funeral
parlor and his casket open wound my mother becomes packs
of cigarettes in his chair in the den where he watched she too
nothing dies shortly thereafter

I was very mad at her because   she had not told me everything
and did she know she used me
        because I stood by stopped breathing too when he walked
scuttling through the living room uncaught
        because I faster than his hand his word he did not catch me
she said he   loved me abstract
she said more than she should had she been good
        would she have turned one day and pulled the dagger
from her apron and   struck how
    could she strike she dreamed for me her dreams extravagant
not of this earth her love too tormented by the way she'd come
to feel he touched he did must have their voices softer must have
meant that and there were not pills not one to help her just my eyes
wired but I had nothing more good mother and she trying

SPLIT

Carol Bruneau

Ethel's house is gone. Men with a crane cut it in two and carted both halves away, making room for a monster house. Our neighbourhood babysitter, Ethel lived there for years with her uncle; she was a big, slow, huge-bosomed woman with white hair and dentures—a separate breed from the bridge-playing, rock-wearing group of housewives who hired her. Of which my mom was a wannabe, sort of, when she wasn't working.

Mom didn't have a diamond but, like most of these mothers, didn't have to work outside the home, for money. Yet, early on, she taught me the value of having a bank account of your own. I'm not sure what the other neighbourhood women did besides cook and clean, bake and tend children. Ethel loved to knit—mitts, hats, scarves for all the kids she minded—like my mom did: tiny sweaters and skirts for my anatomically-sensible Tammy doll. Barbies were barred because they gave a false view of women, Mom said.

She would know, too, being a nurse whose favourite job out of several was at the maternity hospital. The downside for me once I was a teenager, having a mom who'd seen her share of pregnant twelve-year-olds. Her tough warning look was all I needed, sex and the Pill both designed by men as far as she was concerned—my mom who left Betty Friedan's *Feminine Mystique* lying around our gold-and-yellow sixties' living room, like a protest banner, a reminder for everyone to keep in line.

But I'm ahead of myself; let's go back a decade, when our living room was Fifties' green and blue. Because things started for her in

1953 when she married Dad and a few years later had me and seven years after that, my sister—so the egos of husbands and children would dictate, she might say if she could. She's been dead now more than half as long as I've been alive.

But what does this have to do with Ethel? The babysitter who showed up reliably early while Mom raced around getting ready for her 3-11 shifts. Starched cap with black velvet ribbon, white oxfords freshly scuff-proofed, immaculate white pantyhose once pantyhose were invented; oh, the liberation from garters and girdles!

"Ethel," Mom asked one day, probably out of breath, "do you ever wish you'd got married?"

"Maybe for the companionship," was Ethel's simple response.

Maybe the question was for my benefit. Compensation for the time, out of anger—and probably PMS-y frustration over the sticky chaos of kids, my sister's colicky crying, the mess and that whine ("I'm hungry") so irksome to lucky mothers' ears—she had said: "Don't ever get married and if you do, don't ever have kids."

I was too small to take it personally, and years later she absolutely denied saying such a thing: sacrilege. But I distinctly remember rummaging through a tangle of yarn and fabric scraps when she said it, stuff jumbled in a drawer in the spare/sewing/junk/ play room where on rainy days my friends and I built cushion forts—the room which should've been hers, a room of her own. I remember stopping and taking in what she'd said, feeling a bit like some invisible kid or grownup nearby had been slapped while I was somehow exempt. (The way you do when you're innocent and childish enough to think *This will never happen to me.*) Not offended, not hurt, I just felt vaguely confused and guilty—of what, though, I had no idea.

Except, maybe she envied my aunt, one of four sisters in their Cape Breton family of nine, who'd never married, was childless, taught art, painted pictures and travelled the globe. Unlike Ethel, my aunt couldn't even pretend to play the companionship card, having decided at seventeen not to follow in their mother's footsteps, the route my mom had chosen.

"What a shame Bess never married," one of our neighbours said once—maybe just curious but more likely fishing for the *reason*. As if anyone who wasn't married must be seriously defective.

"Are you kidding?" Mom said. "She has a GREAT life."

And still does, Aunt Bess—alive and well and fiercely independent at age 105. Her secret? Not having a man, never having to compromise: that's what she tells the doctors.

But there must've been times mother-and-wifehood weren't onerous for my mom, and were even joyful. Black and white snapshots would attest to these, photos taken by my dad. Mom in a big-sleeved, big-shouldered coat and kerchief, laughing and pulling me on a sled through the snow outside our pretty little white Cape Cod-style home. Mom at the beach, bare-shouldered, shyly beautiful, turning to smile at the camera; a tiny kid in a tartan swimsuit (me) toddling towards her. Just a couple of the countless Kodak Brownie moments recorded; but in my mind are many more: my mom petting her cat, peeling an orange on the picnic blanket, singing over the sink and not cringing a bit as she gutted mackerel—and bigger occasions, like her saying to seven-year-old me writing my first poem: "Maybe you'll be a writer some day." And then there was teaching her neighbourhood friends to drive. Back in those days not all of them knew how—Ethel must've babysat during the lessons—though where we lived you needed a car to get anywhere.

My mother was funny, clever, subversive. Not that being this way made her smug or happy (though I'm sure the satisfaction swung both ways, watching a diamond-ringed friend get her licence and hearing about the husband's surprise). The truth is, my mother would have cherished a diamond ring.

A part of her also loved coffee klatches, bridge parties. She was very social, thrived on being "with the girls." Except that the girlfriends she loved, her real friends, weren't into bridge, diamonds or baking squares. Quite a few were single, mainly colleagues devoted to their hospital jobs. One especially dear one—my godmother—was fiery and outspoken, and might have been a lesbian. Though back then in our little world such a thing was so out there, so hush-hush, it wouldn't've happened. Gayness didn't exist, except when they—my godmother the ringleader—tittered about a doctor who, I learned much later, was in their parlance "a homo." The rest of Mom's circle were "girls" she met doing charity work, collecting and darning clothes for refugees, clothes which she shipped in wooden tea crates cadged from the waterfront cargo sheds and delivered, packed full, to the port in her VW bug.

She always had this busy, altruistic spirit. And she always loved hospitals, though her sisters remember how, as a kid, she fainted at the smell of one.

Her first sweater, knit when she was nine, she donated "to the soldiers" fighting World War II. So maybe it was no surprise when she fell for my dad, a quiet young vet back from overseas. "There's nothing like a fella in a uniform," she told me once, a wistful glint in her eye, when hippie-dippy teens like me turned our noses up at anyone who'd date a crew-cut, not to mention a soldier—well, except for one like my father.

But this story isn't about Dad. Like my sister and me, he was a bystander here. Because my mother's happiest times, I'm convinced, were on the job, nursing—though she'd complain sometimes about snooty doctors and "lazy" new moms, mimicking how, "living the life of Riley" (whoever Riley was), they'd demand to have their beds wound up. She had wicked stories, often meant to shock, well, maybe not shock but startle and warn me about how life could be. Like the story about taking a newborn to the morgue in a flight bag. And the ones from her training on a psych ward, about women who were depressed—women who were problematic—being lobotomized and made "like little kids." Maybe she already knew my writer's heart; maybe she sensed how I was listening, watching, and taking notes as well as taking cues.

"Don't ever be a nurse," she said to me once, in the middle of my grade three concert, the two of us sitting there in the steamy auditorium. (Ethel must've been babysitting my sister.) And in some seismic, illogical way, this was her most baffling, disappointing piece of advice—more startling and much more painful than the one-liner about kids, marriage. *Don't ever be a nurse*—not followed with *Be a Doctor Instead*, or *Be a Teacher like Bess*. Just silence.

The reason it sticks, the reason it stung—a swift sharp slap-upside-the-head—was because I'd seen her at work. On Saturdays when my dad put in overtime at the bank and my aunt couldn't babysit (Ethel didn't do weekends), Mom would take me with her. Imagine. She was working then as an assistant to her best friend, my godmother, who headed the EEG department—a tiny room at the top of the hospital with a machine that traced people's brainwaves in red ink on reams of greenish graph paper. (Like something out of *Bride of Frankenstein*, the electroencephalograph machine makes dot-matrix printers and Commodore 64s seem like Smart phones now, truly.)

It was Mom's job to calm the patients, soothe and reassure them, shave their heads and attach electrodes to the spots on their scalps made by my godmother in red grease pencil. I remember watching while these traumatized souls—sufferers of brain tumours? car crashes? lobotomies?—lay wired up, this machine and its rake-like fingers tracing out the peaks and valleys of their damaged brains' activity. The noise it made was like nails on a chalkboard, a jerky, endless scratching.

Mom and her friend worked quietly, efficiently, then cracked jokes ' between tests. Between patients, they laughed and carried on the way best friends do, and the whole time I would sit there drawing on leftover sheets of graph paper with the nub of a grease pencil. Mostly I remember how perfectly okay and normal it felt to be there watching, as if there were any place else a little girl should be.

It never occurred to me then that anyone suffered or was sick, unhappy, slow, defective, deficient or even different—not in my four-year-old's world. Not back then, before I could read or write, at the tail end of the Fifties. Women were women and they all got along and one day I would be just like them—all of them, this mysterious, amorphous sisterhood. And the squiggly red lines on those sheets and sheets of graph paper weren't brainwaves but marks that interrupted my stick men with their arms and legs growing from heads.

The truth of things didn't dawn till later, once Ethel became a regular at our house, when Mom worked with babies, newborns, "preemies" as she called them, in the hospital nursery. She loved the preemies best, poor helpless, fragile and often damaged beings in their incubators—which, once, in the grocery store, she compared to barbecue chickens. Who knows what Ethel would have made of such a comparison? I suspect Mom would deny making it now— I'm certain she would, had she lived to see my healthy youngest son being incubated briefly in the same hospital, surrounded by nurses she'd worked with and loved. If she'd lived to see any of my kids.

But that's the way things go.

Not long ago, Ethel's obituary appeared in the paper. She lived to a healthy old age, the latter part spent in a nursing home. I imagine she knitted pretty much up till the end, decades after the last of that generation of mothers stopped needing her. They've mostly outlived her, all but one of the ladies my mom taught to drive, and my mother herself, who died too young and too soon of an uncommon neurological disorder, though to the end her heart was strong. She died hating hospitals—left me loving and hating them too, but mostly wondering what it is about brainwaves, how our heads and hearts can be so separate, divided like Ethel's empty house before its removal. A house outlasted by all those around it, though most have changed hands, not a trace remains to show where it stood.

Manhattan

Clarissa Green

From 41st Street, toward
Grand Central Station's sky-swooping arches
seventy years ago
my parents ran laughing to a late train
Manhattan glowing on their exuberant faces.
A night at the theatre
a drink at the Princeton Club
a set of jazz in a neighbourhood with narrow streets.

He wears camel hair, a jacket
clean cut, a soft drape
loafers gleam
in foyer lights
as he guides his girl
down one marble staircase,
then another
her high heels click click click clicking.
Brilliantly, my parents toss themselves into seats.
The train lurches. She laughs,
puts her hand in his hip pocket.

He unscrews the top of a silver flask
offers her a cap full.

In satin and cashmere
a tangle of fox feet dangling
across her breasts, my mother's
wide red smile
invites my father to put an arm around
those rich shoulders of hers.

JEWISH OIL BRAT

Davi Walders

imagine
> *her*

looking through the dusty window,
sand cyclones swirling in the distance
above ten thousand men sleeping in tents,
the endless tracks of the Texas Southern
Pacific and a two-day honeymoon long past,
her eyes large above her swollen belly

imagine
> *longhorns*

snorting at windows she tries to keep
clean, an elm so rare she waters it
growing through the warped floor,
sand hill cranes pecking at lizards
coiled in caleche pits, dogs slower
than armadillos crying in moonless nights

imagine
> *fifteen*

miles from Big Spring, fifteen miles
from nowhere, fifteen frame cottages
resisting the wind, the Settles family
happy to lease to oil squatters
banking green between cactus and
cattle straggling along rutted roads

imagine
     fifty
thousand fenced acres, the Conoco gates opening
for a skinny immigrant of a man,
his *shtetl* Yiddish buried in scholarships
and a deep Texas drawl, his brow already
creased from sun, breaking the rule of dusty
boots, the door slamming behind him

imagine
     the two
of them, ignoring the spotless sky,
the worsening war, whirling through
sand, cactus, and rattlers, holding onto
each other in an old Studebaker, bouncing
by derricks pumping like mules and you,
a *sabra*, about to be born here

---

* sabra: cactus in Hebrew; used to describe first generation born in Israel

BLUE MEDICINE

Maureen Hynes

for the family, a semaphore
of drugstore remedies flashing
in the medicine chest: the menace of Dettol
and the iodine bottle spreading its orange sting
from a nipple-tipped eyedropper,
the oval tin of electric white tooth powder.
But what glows are the medicinal blues,
the eyewash cup like a tiny cobalt trophy,
the laxative bottle,
and for my mother and me, our dry skin,
the squat blue glass jar of Nivea Crème.

Opening the tins and tubes and bottles
is to hear their stories told anew, in loud aromas.
The best bath anticipates the rare ceremony
of the new jar, when my mother peels
off the tinfoil seal and holds
it flat in her hand. I rub the steam
off the mirror and we embrace
cheek to cheek, camera-pose our images
into the beading mirror;
below my curling wet hair and my grin,
the scrawny shoulders and two pale
pennies on my thin chest,
the body that is and is not mine.

Pleased, we disentangle
and she claps the tinfoil sealer
onto my cheek. We display our embrace
to the mirror again: now a full moon
glints silver on my face. I peel it off my cheek
and slap it on hers; we inspect our embrace
again and continue back and forth
until the sealer
no longer sticks.

GETTING READY

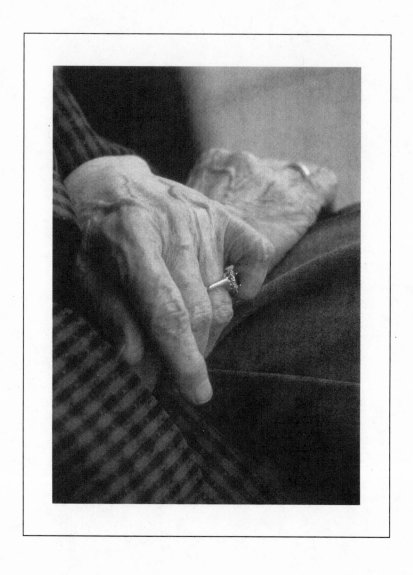

Photo (Grace Glenn's hands): Allan Neilsen (used with permission).

Making Up Mother

Isabel Huggan

I do have a framed photograph of my mother, which sits in a niche by my bedside. Something very peculiar has been happening to it in the last ten years or so, and I study the picture daily to see if this process continues—and it does. Indeed, it seems to be speeding up in a way that alarms and troubles me. Day by day, my mother is getting younger.

When I received it from my father, shortly after her death at age sixty-three, the photograph showed my mother as she was in May 1970, at age fifty-nine, on her one and only trip to California. My father took the shot just after they arrived in their hotel room in San Francisco, a city she had long wanted to visit, ever since her Aunt Margaret (her mother's adventurous sister), had worked there in the '20s and '30s, and had come back to the family farm on the sixth concession with tales of glamour and romance. My mother has a corsage of small, faded pink roses pinned to the lapel of her raspberry-coloured wool suit, and she is smiling in a stiff, unnatural way, as she often did in later years. Her thick, dark hair is cut short, and there is no visible grey, although I am certain she never dyed it. Her brow is slightly furrowed, through the embarrassment of posing for the picture, but her face is unlined, her features fine and even, her blue eyes deep-set and intelligent. An attractive older woman, who had weathered by that point several operations including two rounds of heart surgery, first to clean the mitral valve and then to replace it with a plastic one. She took various drugs after that, including a blood thinner to keep the valve from clogging, and which may have been responsible for the hemorrhagic stroke she suffered in the winter of 1972, which led to her death from another stroke two years later.

I had been married a little over a year and was living in Toronto when my mother had that first stroke. My father phoned the high school where I was teaching to tell me what had happened, and I went directly to the principal with the news that I would be taking a day's leave and would miss a parent-teachers' night scheduled for that evening. He attempted to bully me into staying for the event. "Your mother's not going to die immediately just because she had a stroke," the principal said. "Why, people often linger for *years* afterwards." A stupid, thoughtless man.

I drove that evening to Kitchener where she lay in the hospital, unable to move or speak normally. In the days that followed she regained the power to move her limbs, but her speech was garbled and when she tried to write down what it was she wished to say, her wavery script was indecipherable. Although she had been in hospital many times before, this was different. And she knew it. She understood what had happened, and that made it worse. She had cared for stroke victims during her home-nursing days and, farm girl that she was, had always said: "If I ever have a stroke, take me out to the back forty and shoot me." And now here she was, and no one was going to do that. She was trapped.

Slowly, over the months that followed, she became "nearly herself" again, but there would always be a slight hesitancy in the way she moved and spoke, as though she were not entirely certain that she had said or done something correctly. Her facial expression was often one of a bewildered child who had awakened in the middle of a bad dream, and frequently her face crumpled in frustration. I visited on weekends, and realized as time passed that our relationship was reversing itself: At twenty-nine I had become the mother and she, at sixty-one, the child. In the summer of that year, I drove her up to see her sister Norma in Ripley, and then on to Lake Huron, in hopes that seeing familiar places and people would bring back memories, and indeed it did—but she could not express herself, language kept failing her. Near Kincardine, we sat beneath a tree, holding hands, looking out at the lake and sky, two women by the water's edge, watching the horizon as if for some sign. "I'm not right," she said, as tears slid down her cheeks.

However, she was to make astounding progress in the time she had left. A few years before, the American actress Patricia Neal had had a massive stroke, and her husband, the writer Roald Dahl, organized a rehabilitation program for her with the help of a therapist and the entire English village in which they lived. For several months, following a rigid schedule, a roster of volunteers kept the actress working at fever pitch to recover speech, to relearn language, numbers, concepts, until eventually she was able to return to acting. The success of the scheme was documented in a book, and with this as his guide my father began a similar effort for my mother. Day after day, loyal friends in Elmira came to the house, an hour or two at a time, to prevent Catherine from sinking into depression and to help her do the carefully organized homework laid out for her.

Dad was gentle but firm during this long process, never losing patience as he kept her attention focused on recovery. Every morning, he would write out a page of questions for her to answer before lunch, when he would give her a new set for the afternoon. To begin with the questions were simple—what colour is the sky?—but as the weeks marched on, they became increasingly difficult, drawing upon her memory and knowledge. She'd always loved to play bridge, but after the stroke she couldn't tell a heart from a spade. So the cards would be spread before her, and with help she'd repeat their names until she could go through the deck unaided. By the following year, she could enjoy a game of bridge again, write out a grocery list, carry on a conversation, prepare meals, and lead something like a normal life: but she was increasingly sad, and often spoke of her wish to die so that my father could marry again.

None of my mother's heartache shows in the photo. Only this astounding rejuvenation I see happening, day after day. The older I get—I am her age now—the younger she becomes. She is more youthful in appearance than many of my friends. She looks like the kind of woman I'd want to know better, someone with whom

I might feel comfortable enough to ask intimate questions, and to share my own thoughts and feelings. We could go out—a glass of wine in a café, say—or stay at home with a pot of tea, and really get to know each other. We would have a grand time, and she would tell me everything.

Solo

Marilyn Gear Pilling

A few days before you died you asked me to sing
"The Fairies Make Their Counterpanes" as I'd sung it
at age nine for the Kiwanis Festival. The hospital
bed had been rolled up so you could sit to sleep

for that was the only way you could breathe.
Pillows surrounded you, you looked like a white
queen in a bed of clouds, and though I could no longer
sing, I obeyed your command. You asked me

to stand, to cup one hand inside the other as I'd been
trained to do all those years ago by Mr. Attridge
who came to class three times a week and blew
the opening note on his pitch pipe. Every night,

you put my sister in the playpen beside the piano,
sat down and struck the opening A, then played
the accompaniment, just as Mr. Attridge played it
at school. The song was in the key of G, which means

that F is sharp, but the composer had (perversely)
made one of the F's natural, and I faltered every time
that F natural approached. You isolated the line,
had me sing it over and over and over, 'til my father

ciphering in the kitchen and my brother playing at his
feet wished on the composer an evil fate. When I stood
at the end of your hospital bed and cupped my right
hand inside my left and began in a cracked soprano

to sing *The fairies make their counterpanes from li-ttle
ti-ny threads,* my sister began to cry and my brother,
who was sitting by the window in the only easy chair,
got up and went into the hall. My sister thrust back

the white sheet and the blue counterpane and got into bed
with you and pulled the covers up to her chin. You said,
Get up out of that; what if the nurse comes in!
(for my sister was a doctor in that hospital), and my sister

pulled the covers right over her head. You told me
to start again and you sang a whispery A to start me off
properly. I began, and as I sang of threads and elves and
heather-bells, I thought how the F natural had entered family

lore, how "hitting the F natural" had become a metaphor
known only to those who'd been in that small house
with the Grandma Moses drapes on the picture window
on those winter evenings of 1954, and as I faltered

towards the note for what was surely the last time,
my heart saw us with a clarity that was unsought—
my sister in bed beside you, my brother, visible, but more
in the hall than the doorway, my father, a mile down

the road in the nursing home six weeks from his own death,
you, the white queen with the blue tinge on her lips,
and me, reluctant soloist headed for some limbo between
F natural and F sharp—and I thought

how the skein that held us had thinned to flimsiest gossamer,
how the merest breath would take it,
how intricate its weave as it floated away,
how outrageous its unravelling.

GETTING READY

Lynda Monahan

when they told her
it was terminal
i remember thinking
it was like she was taking a trip
somewhere
& wanted to make sure
everything was looked after
while she was away

she showed me how
grandpa liked his tea
extra strong three sugars
where to go
to pay the power bill
how often to water the houseplants

getting ready to go
as if any minute
she would be packing up her suitcase
with her two good dresses
having dad drop her off
at the bus terminal
clutching a packet of peppermints
for the ride
with a nickel in her jacket pocket
to call home
from the other end

EXTENDED CARE

Rhona McAdam

We did as we were taught
by you. Nursing home, the place
where mothers go: yours, his.

But they changed, those places.
Nurses, yes. They put a capital letter
in Home, and that made a difference.

You who forgave us everything
forgave us even this.

A room without walls.
Someone else's shoes
on your feet. Waking
to find someone circling your bed,
fingering your clothes,
opening your dresser drawers.

Mornings sat in a circle
with dead-eyed women nudging a ball
you wouldn't touch,
eyeing that window (locked).
Locked doors. Elevators so slow
you could die by the time
you reached bottom. Locked doors
between you and the garden.
You in the lounge of the living dead.

Finding change in your pocket
to call your husband
like you used to when you were lost,
tell him: come and get me;
ask him: when will you join me here?

Taking your place in the lounge
to watch the ambulances
roll up to the doors
with their random loads.
Incoming. Outgoing. Nothing moves
but your eyes. Something gone missing.

THE NIGHT SHE DIED

Lekkie Hopkins

I wasn't there. I'd planned to come the next weekend, to give my brother and his wife a break. She'd been with them almost a month, relishing the care they gave, determined this would only be an interlude.

The last time I had seen her we talked of heartbreak and of many things besides—of books she loved, family stories, music. Easy talk, intermittent, threading its way through long afternoons of plumping pillows, slanting light; through evenings and nights where the only sounds were the curlew's call and the slough of the sea, sighing.

That time I told her about the painting I'd bought at an exhibition. Violet and Ochre, it's called. It's big, I said, and beautiful. The artist is a man whose name I did not know: Chen Ping. His grandfather's a painter, traditional, and migration made him want to blend the strokes from East and West. I told her then about the work, its bold brushstrokes, its energy. Two figures take up all the space. The violet figure's tall and poised, right arm raised above the head, left arm graceful at the waist, just so. At first the violet's all the eye can see. But as you stand and stare, from left of field you see a splash of ochre. Then another, more and more till you see a twirling dervish. My girls. My mother laughed, remembering that as children one was dark and poised, obedient and charming, the other gold and freckled, never still. I bought it to remind me of a mother's love, I said.

The night she died she called me. Just want to let you know that Doctor says I needn't fight this evil any more. Hospital, he says, is what comes next. But I don't want to go. I'm happy here at home. Oh Mama mine, I had said, we'll sort it out. I'll see you soon—on Friday. Can we talk about it then? Right now I have some neighbours here to help me hang my painting.

The night she died she called my sister too. They chatted for a while of this and that, and then hung up.

The night she died my brother and his wife suspected nothing, though she'd called them both into her room, insisting that they stay: No, don't go, dear, until I fall asleep.

The night she died I slept the sleep of angels—deep and clear and long. At six I woke and heard myself give three long sighs—Aahh! Aahh! Aahh! I stretched and turned, luxuriating, then drifted off again. At seven I stumbled out of bed to get the phone. I thought, Oh dear Mama. And sure enough, my brother's voice, bewildered, cracking. Bad news, love. She's gone. She passed away an hour ago. I know, I said, bewildered too. I know.

Apartment 1422

Allison Marion

The faded beige walls are marked with randomly-placed white ghost windows, as if someone had painted them that way. Only weeks ago, a photo display of her children and grandchildren lay over those white squares though, sadly, one of me and my family was not among them. A thin wooden book case at the entrance now holds only scatterings of dust. A musty 1930s cedar chest, emptied of memories, sits in the bedroom with its lid open as if to breathe in much-needed fresh air.

No more knick-knacks. These were packed up weeks ago, shortly after she died. Some of these my siblings kept, others we gave away to charity, and some we discarded. That was hard to do. How do you decide? Who has the right to decide? A pinwheel flower vase used only for special occasions, her cherished Silver Birch china set or a crystal candy dish, filled with vibrantly-coloured jelly beans during the holiday season; these became part of her.

Before she lost her eyesight her vast collection of books was always lined up neatly on the shelf, within reach. Her oak rocking chair took prominence in the living room. It was her sanctuary, a place of comfort, respite from the growing pain. And let's not forget the radios. I can't tell you how many radios there were in these three small rooms; we lost count. She had succumbed to macular degeneration in her later years, and lost her sight. As the years wore on, radios and the television became her lifeline. CBC news, the 40s swing music blaring from Benny Goodman's clarinet, the ongoing and unpredictable Manitoba weather updates: these were the sounds of her sheltered world.

On a bitterly cold January evening I arrived, reluctantly, with her apartment keys in hand, knowing it would be the last time I would enter these rooms. The building manager had been waiting for the keys; I had put it off for weeks. I mustered up the courage, opened the door, and stopped, startled by the chill. The window: she had always kept the kitchen window open just a crack to mask her cigarette smoke; and of course it never worked. The furniture, the dishes, the towels—everything smelled of smoke. It still did.

Outside the living room window, the lights on Fermor Avenue blinked as cars whizzed by, headlights illuminating the frost on the inside panes of glass. The faded blue brocade drapes hung listless. I remember how happy she was when she bought those drapes, how they matched her colour scheme of Wedgewood blue and ivory. As I made my way to the kitchen, the icy breezes felt sharper. I was shivering. I reached into my jacket pocket, grabbed my gloves, and leaned over the sink, struggling to shut the old aluminium window. The leverage wasn't there so I propped myself up onto the kitchen counter, yanking at the window until my arms hurt.

Shoot, nothing. No luck. The cold air poured in.

How did she ever manage to close that? Her obituary described her as a tough and resilient Scot. Well, she was; no frozen window ever got the best of her. She was only five feet and no more than 90 pounds by the end. In the last few months, on days when her stomach would welcome food, her diet had consisted of three foods: ice cream (mainly vanilla), Jell-O (any flavour would do) and cream of chicken soup, at any hour of the day, and in no particular order. The cancer had whittled away her small frame pound by pound.

Well, forget it then, I said aloud. The building manager will just have to deal with it.

The bedroom at the end of the hall was nearly bare. In a happier time, a blue feather duvet would have been neatly draped on her bed beside the cheap white French Provincial-style dresser. After her divorce, she took possession of that dresser from me, filling it with her own mementos. When my brothers and sister and I cleaned it out, we discovered secrets and mysteries, some of which we will never know the answers to, and some we were shocked to discover. A faded black and white picture of her and her first love standing beside a rusty old 1940s car. Her white gold wedding rings: why were the diamonds chiselled out of their settings? Beside the dresser, the 60-year-old cedar chest, leather straps parched and faded, sat waiting for a new owner.

As I walked back to the living room past the storage closet, I remember the cardboard shoe boxes we had discovered high on the top shelf. One box for each of her four children, their full given names shakily printed in thick black marker, with instructions not to open until after she was gone. They were haphazardly taped, as if she was in a hurry to finish them. It must have been a difficult task for those 85-year-old hands, crippled and thickened with arthritis, and those eyes, which only saw a glimmer of light.

Afraid of what might be in the box meant for me, I had waited a few days after she died to open it. It was no secret to anyone who knew us that she and I had rarely seen eye to eye during our difficult 53-year relationship. Marriage, my child-rearing capabilities, education, and the length of my hair were always among the top ten in our mother-daughter arguments. Her painful and gut-wrenching divorce years had torn a hole in her heart, and in mine. At a time when a daughter should be there to support her mother, I was shocked and angry when my father's lawyer subpoenaed me to be a witness. Wanting to be Switzerland in the courtroom, I carefully avoided answering the difficult questions; the judge declared me a hostile witness. I don't think my mother and I ever recovered from that day in court. So when I saw the shoebox with my name on it, I was surprised. What could she possibly have left for me?

One day, after a long conversation with my brother and sister over a bottle of wine, they persuaded me to go ahead and open it.

"If you don't, we will," they taunted, more excited or curious than I was, it seemed. "In her own way, she did love you. She couldn't tell you how she felt because you wouldn't listen. This is her way of showing you." I relented.

What she left for me was indeed a reminder of how beautiful she was. Items I had given her when I was a child were wrapped in faded tissue paper and arranged carefully inside. I gingerly took the wrapping from each item: the colourful ceramic ashtray crafted at my first ceramics class; the costume jewellery earrings bought at the Saskatoon Woolworth's store when I was fourteen; the faded construction paper birthday cards. Some of those gifts now sit in my own bookcases.

It was late, and I heard the cold wind against the kitchen window. I pulled the keys from my pocket, wiped away tears, and closed and locked the apartment door. The silence was filled with the memory of jingling chimes that always hung from that door, alerting her to visitors. As it always had, the door closed with a slam. Who would be the next tenant? Would they open the kitchen window a tiny crack to allow cool fall breezes in, or to mask the smell of smoke? Would they reconcile with their daughter before the years got the best of them?

The elevator ride down to the main floor seemed to last an eternity. I wondered if I would have any occasion to enter this building again. I found the manager's door and knocked, then waited a bit before knocking again. After a minute or so, I wandered around the lobby to look for him.

Circling back to his door, I saw the buzzer. How did I miss that?

No answer. I buzzed again. Nothing.

Zipping up my parka, I walked slowly through the vestibule doors and into the quiet dark of the visitor parking lot. I stood there for a moment remembering better times when I would park the car, wait for her to come downstairs so we could go to my son's baseball game, go shopping, savour an ice cream cone in the park. I turned and looked up to the 14th floor window for a moment, my face wet with snow falling cool against my face.

It's been nearly five years since her passing, and to this day, the keys to apartment 1422 are still on my keychain.

THIRD *YAHRZEIT*

Davi Walders

Perhaps, this May, I'll let azaleas burst
into fuchsia bloom, the dogwoods shimmer
into white, and not hide from rivers loosed

from rocky beds and ice. Perhaps this May
I'll watch stamen rise and curl like snails,
peeking from soft petalled pink, not crumpled

brown, withered, wet, like salted slugs that
stained my arm as I banged an almost-orphaned
knee on metal crank and air-conditioned ledge

oozing onto straws and gauze long gone. Perhaps
this May I will protect those knees, these arms,
other extremities—not zip into a blue-curtained

womb and let flat tracks flash me back to cotton
pods, refinery smoke, bayous red and brown,
nor fly a thousand miles to walk beneath grey

Spanish moss where sprinklers swished a spiral
noose on names and dying grass, nor let myself
retrace that loss on a shining marble slab

or leave another smaller stone, as though things
once unveiled could be contained by pebbles,
weights. Perhaps this May no one will come

to pray, the house will lose its echo, the deli smell
of pickled fish, the scent of potted plants,
bedded in foil and bows. Perhaps I will forget

each hatchet phrase, *"She was ready," "God called
her," "Get a dog," "Just stay busy."* Perhaps this
spring I'll simply mark the time by sitting

in a park or in a kitchen newly painted pink,
a room without a wheelchair, pain, and let
the shadows play. Perhaps I'll hear a leaf

brush the window screen, a cardinal in the yard,
then say Kaddish as the wick begins to flame,
or perhaps this year I'll just pour a glass

of wine, lift crystal stem towards light,
press lip against my lips and sip in quiet
peace before I whisper, *"l'Chayim."*

MY MOTHER'S NAME WAS NANCY

Lynda Monahan

she wore red lipstick pinched her cheeks to give
them colour after the war mom met a young frenchman
who broke her heart   later she married dad
in a long satin gown   fifty tiny buttons down her back

her favourite sister was the oldest   jessie
mom visited her in toronto not long before she died
she bought two new dresses   one a butter yellow
the other bright blue   she was buried in the yellow dress
the one she liked best

she grew glorious roses   lush gardens of fat vegetables
her cold room shelves lined with gem jars of canned
crabapples   sewed red velvet dresses for my sister and i
short pants for our brother   made her own mastectomy bras
stuffing them with old stockings

she kept four geese   herman and hector   pansy and petunia
they'd stampede up the driveway and we'd make a run
for the door   closing it fast on their snapping beaks
they adored mom though   coming when she called
rubbing their wings against her legs

she loved wandering the woods back of our house
made bottle gardens from moss and seedlings   sold them
in the craft shop at the lake   miniature replicas of the
nisbet forest   the place that was her home

she baked terrible pies using margarine in the crust
wonderful cakes from her best friend's recipe   coo clark's
crazy chocolate cake   she liked readers digest condensed
versions   big leathery brown volumes special ordered
through the mail   lost herself in stories like *the slow
awakening*   curled in an armchair in a pool of lamplight
head tilted to one side

she learned to drive in her forties   stalled the car in
the middle of second avenue once   thought it was my fault
because i closed the ashtray she never took a drink
wouldn't dance   seldom missed church
and that was the one time i heard her say *damn*

when she lost her hair she wore a brown wig
squeezed a rubber ball to help her regain strength
in her arms   though it never returned
she could hardly lift a thing but she climbed up
and fixed the eaves on the house   and when she did
dad wouldn't speak to her for three days

she stayed home as long as she could   showing me
how to make seven layer dinner   when to add the
fabric softener   two weeks before christmas   in the middle
of the night dr. martinson   came
saying   *nancy its time we took you to the hospital now*
and she hesitated   then her quiet voice answered him   *yes*

BORDERS

Eve Joseph

My mother liked black coffee with Cointreau. She liked the way the liqueur swirled like a thin film of oil on water before it disappeared. I imagine if I had asked her she would have had a story to tell about the taste of Spain's bitter orange peels. Her stories rarely had a beginning or an end. They started in the middle of a thought or memory as if she was suddenly speaking from some other place. Years after the war a shell fragment pushed its way out through her eyebrow; the entry wounds were invisible but the evidence was compelling. Her stories were much like that.

Slowly the shape of the garden emerged.

A shape, mom, which emerged out of other gardens. The secret one you played in as a child on the Isle of Wight; the wild expanse of heather on the moors where you rode alone most mornings.

Books were read, fertilizers were studied. Many discussions, many points of view were offered. By the following spring, daffodils, tulips, rock gentian took hold of the prepared beds.

I look up gentian and find that the most precious are the perennial alpines from the Alps. You spend days on your knees planting these little mountain flowers in your garden on the coast.

Lily of the Valley found its own niche and was able to pretend it wasn't there. Clarkia and larkspur followed.

Clarkia, otherwise known as ragged robin, deerhorn, elkhorn. Did you know the plants you referred to as the shy, gentle ones were also known as pink faeries? When you told me there were faeries at the foot of the garden was it the truth I heard in your voice that caused me to be lost to the world of water babies and the diaphanous? Was it your certainty that led me to line match boxes with soft grasses: to place them beneath the nasturtiums and check them in the morning for the faintest of imprints?

Trees, bushes arrived as gifts from the unknown: from other caring gardeners. One, in particular, a tiny Japanese Maple.

Simon Ortiz says there are no truths, only stories. Storyteller, that's what you were. For over thirty years you lived with Leslie and Colleen, two women with Down Syndrome. One week before you died, the Philippine woman who came to bathe you arrived in her wedding dress: white with gossamer frills scalloped down her back. Colleen disappeared upstairs and re-appeared wearing her strap-on wings from Halloween. In the photo you took of them they look weightless like Chagall angels.

Chagall prayed: *Will God or someone else give me strength to breathe the breath of prayer and mourning into my paintings?*

In reality it was you floating away.

The tiny Japanese Maple grew big and strong. Forty-five years later it leans protectively over a canary yellow azalea. A special gift.

History's transmogrifications. I grew up believing my brother had given it to you as a mother's day gift. In my memory, it was the one living thing that remained of him. My sister tells me it was a gift from her boyfriend. She and Al stood in the bluebells and necked below the kitchen window where you couldn't see them.

Delphiniums thrived along with their cousins—pelargoniums. From the palest pink to the scarlet of a Mountie's dress uniform.

It's hard work this morning, mom. I feel everything tinged by too much sweetness. You hated August. The garden moribund, fleshy. The sweltering heat and decay: a listlessness to the days. It was the one month of the year that uncloaked you; that laid bare your shell-shocked soul.

In Shanklin you won a contest for the brownest back on the Island. In a photograph fifty years later, transfixed, you gaze out across the Solent from a hotel window. Not still images in your eyes, but moving pictures. Images flashing and tumbling over one another. You were a young woman in London during the war; the girl in you never left the Island.

The tiny house was beginning to establish itself with some intensity but this is the story of the garden and the house with all its growing pains—joy, sadness, tragedy, despair, hope—must wait for another time.

Elbow to elbow, we shared the house with John and Ian. It didn't matter that they were ghosts. John brought the sea: the arterial waterways of war; the shores of breathless reunion. He was Cairo and Alexandria; he was Malta. He was the signature in the left hand corner of the watercolour—the wooden rowboat and the loosely draped grapevines. He was your love.

It doesn't seem so long ago when John said: "Take the ferry at the bottom of Lonsdale, turn right and you will come to the Marine building. Go to the 17th floor and I'll be there. And he was, with all his adoring love. And then he died.

You wrote in your favourite restaurants. A carafe of Chilean wine with your meal, two shots of Cointreau with your coffee. Everywhere you went people fell in love with you. Once I stood across the street from the Orange Club on Lonsdale and watched you at your table by the window. A glimpse, mom, of how slow pleasure can be.

So forgive me this mourning for once again there is death. The second one just as lonely as the first.

The right side of your face is bathed in lamplight, the left in shadow. The phone is in your hand only you're not talking into it; you're holding it away from your face and your words are not making sense. Decades later, reading, *I sensed an infinite scream passing through nature,* by Edvard Munch, I recognize that your grief at your son's death was inseparable from the infinite. It reverberated through your nerve endings into the night sky. It howled along a stretch of highway thousands of miles away. It entered me and became a permanent vibration. Dylan's *ghost of electricity* howling through the bones of your face.

The garden was settling in for winter, no great changes were visible but the next spring it became obvious that something was different. The beloved garden had overstepped its city boundaries. The flower beds had spread over the sidewalk, especially the rambling plants: bleeding heart, winter jasmine, gentian with all its shades of blue; ferns lavender, rununculus, iris and on and on.

The old block was changing. When the last of the houses came down across the street and the last of neighbours had gone, you planted a row of quaking aspens in the front garden to hide the townhouses; or as you called them *the abortions.*

You told me a woman in a long white dress came to you. She walked toward you from a great distance and only when she was close did you recognize her as your mother. What, I wonder, did she see? The child or the old woman? You looked me right in the eye and asked *does this mean I will die soon?*

There was no resistance in you, no line left to tether you. You were floating, still here on earth, floating.

Of all the restaurants, Loops was your favourite. From your table you could see sparks flying from the ships in dry-dock. You watched Cates tugs nosing freighters in and out of the piers and Seaspan barges fill their decks with their pyramids of sawdust. You waited at your table in the sun.

Maybe the death of Loops is the last of my deaths, when the last one will be mine and all these deaths will be worthwhile and Mark, David, Michael, Darryl, Kathy, Samia and the bread boys will greet me again.

I'm becoming a gardener, mom. Last year I planted slender yellow lilies and Japanese Iris. Your old bike is leaning up against the cedar tree. This year I will plant nasturtiums in the basket. The garden is beginning to shape itself. *It was then that all the deaths came alive and once again I was dancing and all the deaths were not deaths but memories and Harry with his quartet plus his gifted, and not so gifted pianists, will struggle once more with A Nightingale Sang in Berkley Square.*

[*Note:* This piece was written following my mother's death. The italicized lines are her journal entries]

WEEDING, LATE SUMMER

Sue Chenette

Quack grass by the handful,
twist and yank, roots
gripped in summer-dry clay,
broken stems tossed onto the lawn.

My mother and I are trying to reorder
the backyard raspberry patch.
We tackle the dandelions,
nudging an angle-weeder
down along tap-roots.
It's bent, swivels,
yields only broken stubs.

A spade, then?
But what we'd wish away—
rooted deep as old grievances—
grows so closely intertwined
with bearing canes, their branches
loaded now, that we can't dig
without damage. Nothing for it

but to leave old stubble
and roots.
               And these
late summer asters, purple fringe
overspreading a southwest corner.

Wearing My Mother's Dresses

Cynthia Woodman Kerkham

> *Thou art thy mother's glass, and she in thee*
> *Calls back the lovely April of her prime.*
> "Sonnet 3," William Shakespeare

At your funeral, I wore the chocolate cocktail dress
tied at the waist with the rolled cord;
sis chose one of your beaded sweaters;
Auntie Claire, the Chanel suit—

a tribute to your walk-in closet,
how you tailored your girls
in yellow-checked gingham sprung wide with crinolines,
velvet smocks with white collars,
elbow-length gloves, sashed blue dancing frocks.

Your red ballroom gown,
heavy silk with beaded bodice,
I'll sheathe in cleaner's plastic, hold on to.

I fit the mocha lace
A-line, the one scalloped at hem,
cuffs and collarbone,

I'll throw parties just to wear it.

Remember the green and white floral number,
how its wide skirt taffeta-shushed as you passed me
getting ready to go out? I'd follow you,
bury my jammy face in its glossy folds

and when you were gone, I'd sneak

into your cupboard

clomp in your pink velveteen heels,
silver brocade dress,
swing a stole around my shoulders.

In your full-length glass,
watch myself twirl: embroidered stars, black shot silk.

YOUR HANDS

Cynthia French

February, 1992

I ease you from the half tub in the cramped closet bathroom at St. Clare's. You feel brittle, as if bones, muscles, sinew, and even body fluids have somehow hardened. I am filled with an irrational fear that a sudden movement might snap you in two. You vibrate—a rage inside you, your jaw is clenched, and you are fighting—but I know it isn't a battle to live. I watched you earlier in the hospital bed scratching at your wrists with your thumbnail in a futile demented attempt to die. I'd hoped the warmth of the water, the ritual cleansing might ease your distress. But you are stripped of any comfort. Dis-ease. Arthritis has tormented you for years. Is this what has eaten away at you? That disfigurement and a deeper pain borne of striving for unreachable domestic perfection? Once I was the nervous sickly child with skinny arms and legs, distended belly. It was I who needed soothing and you who were bathing me.

You lift us in and out of the tub. Your hands soap and rinse and you sing "It's a Long Way to Tipperary." "Pack up Your Troubles in your Old Kit Bag." (Your favourite cousin, Jimmy, handsome face in a frame on your bureau, killed in the war). "Mairzy doats and dozy doats and liddle lamzy divey." And on the bathroom windowsill, the unnamed, pinkish-red rubber gadget—a peculiar toy—ridged hollow ball with hose attached. No pill then, you manage to space out our births. All girls, we arrive in 1942, '45, '52 and '56. In between, a miss. What other methods of birth control did you have? Twin beds—wedding gifts from your mother-in-law—she of the double bed and eight children. Rhythm. Withdrawal. A headache.

No disposables—you rinse cloth diapers in the toilet. Your hands dip up, down, up, down, scrub, flush, then wring, wring, wring out the water, ice-cold. Some nights, your fingers stroke keys, Chopin or Strauss waltzes float up the stairs as we doze off. By the time my babies come, your hands—knuckles swollen, wrists weak—can no longer carry your grandchildren.

Your hands make secrets—you bar off the kitchen door with the pulled-over drawer. The mixer whirring. Scent of vanilla, lemon, almond. Cherry or chocolate cake or my favourite—a four-layered concoction with mushy pineapple filling and gooey boiled icing. On birthdays we are excused from chores, surprise gifts are wrapped, waiting by our place. Wishes rise in the waxy smoke.

You stand on your feet for hours, ironing sheets, blouses, napkins, place mats, dish towels, Dad's handkerchiefs and undershorts. Steam builds up as you fold, smooth, sprinkle, reach for a puff of your Matinee, veins spidering up your calves, purpling, knotting. But trying on the new clothes you've brought up on appro from Ayre's or The London, New York and Paris you parade in front of the long mirror in the hall, then break into dance, *Five-Foot-Two, Eyes of Blue*. You criss-cross hands to knees, heel, toe, front, back, sideways. You cut a mean Charleston, your legs kick high and easy.

You sit by the telephone—classic black, dial models—one in the front hall, the other by Dad's side of the bed. Twenty-five-second calls to Murphy's on the Cross—*Miss O'Toole—add a box of Bon Ami and two tins of Horsey Orange Juice to my order.* Hour-long calls to your friends, Peg, Judy, or Hick, doodling women's heads on an envelope, *um-hmm*, in-drawn breath, *yeah, yeah, um-hmm.* Woman-talk, mysterious, cryptic.

Your fingers wind wool on steel needles, as you knit endless tube socks for children in Nain. The knit two, purl two pattern is simple so you watch the new television. Rabbit ears, black and white, two channels. Sunday nights, Princess, Bud, and Kitten's mother Betty smiling in her spotless frock, clean house. Father solving every problem in half an hour, minus commercials. The formula for perfection—whiter whites, shinier floors, lighter cakes, chirpier children, happier husbands—reflecting on the surface of your eyes. On your chintz chair arm are magazines with glossy covers—*Good Housekeeping, Ladies Home Journal,* and the enticing Canadian version, *Chatelaine*—recipes for jellied salads, articles like "How to Wash Down the Walls, Be Dressed and Fresh when your Man Comes Home for Dinner."

You spend one night a month at your desk doing your 'accounts', reconciling, writing cheques, paying bills. One year in a spurt of daring you order a bunch of summer clothes from Eaton's catalogue. The morning they arrive we're excited—t-shirts, shorts, pedal-pushers, all in the latest stripes and plaids. That night, Dad looks at the bill, lays down the law: *send the whole lot back.* Fifty years later, my older sister is still bitter.

Last thing every night, milk bottles are placed on the step, tickets stuck in the necks. In the morning, top milk, cream, is poured off and saved for your cereal. You seldom come down until after we've left for school.

Some nights you sit brooding at the table, your lip out a mile. We are tense with waiting. Your body seems to vibrate as you jump up, storm from the kitchen. *I'm going to kill myself. You'll be sorry.* Every time I hear the front door slam behind you I think, *it's my fault, if I could only be better, not cranky, not 'high-strung'.* My stomach aches with the worry that this time you might not come home.

A weird electricity thrums through your body—foreign, destructive. You are so strung out you're not bothered that I have never before seen you naked. You pace on the spot. I hurry to dry you, caught between the need to be gentle and to get this over. I towel off your wasted body; shoulders, back, rib cage, legs, feet, forget between your toes. You gnaw at your lip, knobby fingers pick at the towel in distress. I take your bent and twisted hands between mine, try to hold them still, pat them dry. I do not have the strength to sing.

DEVIL'S APRON

Lorri Neilsen Glenn

Jennifer injects the morphine, pauses at the end of the bed, jaw set, eyes down. They will sometimes stop breathing for thirty seconds, she says, then start up again. Or sit bolt upright, look at you with complete awareness, and fall back. Two minutes with no breath is when they call it.

The sea hisses, booms. The tide is too high to walk on the beach, so we pick our way over the tumble of icy rocks, the kelp slippery under our feet. Mid-afternoon and the sun is already low. He is pointing at the water. I see his mouth move, but can't hear. I tie my hood more tightly, squint as the ocean rises, writes the end of its heaving in ragged white lines, spindrift and spume.

My sister was here this time last year, so I understand.

In this hospital? I ask. Your sister? She nods. My own sister, sitting on the other side of the bed, blinks slowly, shakes her head. Jennifer is so young.

Last week, in X-ray, my mother's bones were a crumpled clothesline under the Johnny shirt, her legs trembling, barium drool running like melted ice cream off her chin to splash on the worn tiles. C'mon Mom, I urged from behind a screen. One more swallow.

Jennifer rests her hand on Mom's foot. Has she spoken? Not today, I say. Last night, Beverley came in with an aide to turn her, and she held out her arms. *Oh, I love you, I love you!* Beseeching. A word from the same root as 'seek.'

You know she's blind, I say. Not all the nurses know. Now she's confused too. I realize I am talking about my mother in the third person. Can she hear?

The shoreline white as cloud. White as my breath against a rimy window in a small Northern town decades ago, as scurf under my fingernail when I scratch the glass. In the back yard, piles of snow around a circle. My father running the hose; the surface freezing into ice bones that snag my toe picks. No matter; at seven, I could twirl, I was sure, like Sonja Henie on the screen on Saturday afternoon. Glory on ice.

My boot slides on the loops of kelp; he grabs my arm. Mustard brown—no, baby poop yellow, perhaps, or dark ochre. Gold rubber bands, twisting inside themselves; Möbius gone mad, sprawled along the beach. Devil's apron. I hold out a glistening strip to him, but he only smiles. Laminaria bulbosa: I learn later it can be used in birth, to dilate the cervix. Dried, it takes on water, and swells.

It doesn't matter, says Allison. My sister, her left hand against her nose, is taking her turn on the side of the bed next to a biliary machine that will be turned off today. All that matters is that it was someone she thought she loved.

We are the only ones on the beach. Two Sunday walkers, childbirth long behind us. I still wonder how she knew. Thirty years ago, my lungs desperate for air, and the forceps ready in the doctor's hands. My husband's voice: your mother is on the phone, long distance. From three provinces away? Later: I just had a sense, she said. Sometimes you just know.

Mom, we're here, I say. Periodically, one of us leaves to find a fresh washcloth, lay it on Mom's forehead, dampen her dry lips. Outside, I can see smokestacks billow white sheets into the air and across the way cars fret back and forth on the Maryland Bridge. Why so much traffic this morning? Someone out for coffee cream, perhaps.

A family with wrapped packages on their way, a single person driving home from a party.

Outside it is 40 below. The Manitoba sky is the texture and colour of harbour ice. It was only yesterday that she was moved from the ward to the last room, still alert. Hello Grace, the doctor on call had said, offering his hand. I'm the palliative care physician.

Jesus Christ, she said, and fell back on the pillow. When her friend came later in the day, she crooned, *Oh, I love you Millie*, and reached from the bed like a child wanting up.

At the edge of the beach, rocks emerge like black eggs from shells of shore ice. A moonscape, a winter we have to navigate. How is it that, even after years, we can call forth a memory as though we are still there? The wind stings my bare hand as I grasp the kelp. What are you doing with that, he asks, as we turn toward the car.

Look at this colour against the bright red, I say, and I lay the devil's apron across the hood of the car, thinking: I am stealing a string of ocean memory.

I give up my chair to my brother. In the corridor the nurses have set up a coffee stand under mistletoe and crepe paper streamers. An elderly woman with rheumy eyes sits in her wheelchair, a red tissue crown from a cracker tipped sideways over her sparse white hair, the thin elastic impressing her cheek. The staff lounge table is filled with bright wrapping, open boxes of candy. The elevator dings: heavy boots and thick coats and chatter. I pour a coffee, search for a spoon.

No more words now. Just breathing. For days she had picked at the sheets frantically, rubbed and scratched her head, begged me to cut off her hair. We found her naked in the bed, jumpy, her smooth limbs and back glowing in their own pale light. *Would you tell them there is no need for the militia*, she said once, hearing visitors in the corridor.

Last week—was it only?—we brought in popsicles and she had whooped with delight. The day after, scotch. We closed the curtains, poured a few drops on a teaspoon, and watched her drowsy eyes pop open. *Oh my—I'll have more of that.*

Back at the house, I startle the chickadees as I toss mouldy bread off the stoop for the gulls and the deer. Inside, he fills the wood stove, now down to coals. From the window, grey water, white caps, the wink of devil's apron, hanging alone in the branches. Above it, cedar waxwings, like pen nibs, lift and drop. Lift and drop.

I wanted to see how it dries, I tell him.

Oh, Mom. For hours that morning, those were the only words I could speak. Three days before, on the winter solstice, her ex-husband's heart stopped. We drove in the ice fog across the city to another hospital, said good-bye to our father as he was given last rites, and drove back across the bridge to hallways lined with paper snowflakes, blinking lights, gold ribbons on plastic trees.

He's dead, isn't he, she asked the morning after, although none of us had said. *Leave me alone for a few minutes.* She covered her face, and I closed the curtain around the bed.

I pour a fresh cup of coffee, sit and watch the waves in the bay for a few moments. The gulls and crows have long since devoured the bread in the yard. The sun is gone. Student papers lie on the table beside me. I rub my hands, still cold from our walk, notice how thick my knuckles have become.

Those thick knuckles. That last night, when all four of us were in the room, she sat up, eyes closed, clasped her arms around the nearest one, each of her children in turn. Then she flopped back. Last burst, it's called. Like false labour: death's Braxton Hicks.

She won't see Jean, I thought. Her childhood friend, a cousin from Strathclair, had called the hospital when Mom was admitted and somehow, the staff cannot bring a portable phone to her bedside. Is it enough that we have called Jean ourselves, and have told Mom this? Is it enough we have called her brother—*he's so goddamned stubborn*—and, even though he has refused to visit, have told her, bending the truth a bit, that he wishes his sister the best? And the man who left her twenty years ago for his secretary—my father, the cliché—now gone. We are down to one room—four children, and a mother—on Christmas morning.

Her body is hot, as though cooking itself from inside, her skin jaundiced and clammy. I stroke the side of her forehead and cheek. Allison holds the fingers of Mom's hand, resting her own free hand on Mom's heart.

A song is on the player in the room. "O Holy Night," again. Then, "O Mio Babbino Caro." "Nessun Dorma." Swells and a tenor. My brother's dark hit parade. For the first time, I understand opera.

The Golden Boy on top of the Legislature glints, but only dimly; the sky is overcast. I am so far away from the sea.

O notte. Tramontate stelle. I rinse another washcloth under cold water and with a couple of fingers under the cloth, I begin slowly, carefully to wipe Mom's face and chest. *A burning forehead, a parching tongue.* She takes in one deep breath, then shudders. Another, and her chest falls. She is still. Allison's eyes widen.

One corner of Mom's mouth lifts, a small almost-smile. Is she conscious? I wipe her cheek, her neck, and undo the top button of her nightgown to reach her collarbones. I'd helped her buy it one winter at The Bay in the local mall. She'd plopped down on a pile of boxes near the changing room while I wove in and out of racks to find an easy-to-button housedress. This one had smocking and buttons. Cornflower blue. Take it; that's good enough, she said. Let's go. And I'm paying; so don't try. And don't argue.

I open the folder, take out a paper. Last week in class Tiffany had said to me: that's a funky strand of red in your hair. Is that new?

We'll take you to Strathclair, Mom, I say, wringing out the washcloth and adding more cool water. We'll take you to be with Aunt Laura, with your dad, with Aunt Bell. We'll drive you past the old Green Bluff School. Jean will be there.

Once again I remove the cloth, now warm, to rinse it in cold water. It's then I notice.

Her left eye is dry with a stare that reaches beyond anywhere we can see. But her right eye is bright. It is brimming with tears that cling to her lower lashes.

It's the time of year, I told Tiffany. A marker. A memory I keep when winter is on its way.

Her chest lifts. One breath more.

WATER TO WATER

Margaret M. Zielinski

My mother loved to swim:
crippled by arthritis she could only hobble
down to the lake's edge,
cane in hand, and holding hard the opposing hip,
sigh and slide her feet, carefully—she dare not slip—
among the pebbles scattered on the sloping sand.

I'd watch as, waves to waist, she'd turn
and toss her cane to shore and dive away beneath the lake
to glide through floating fronds of weeds,
and stroke through water,
warm and welcoming,
smooth as moonlight on her skin.

And I'd think how once we crawled from water,
and to water are at last released.

ACKNOWLEDGEMENTS

"Happy and Lucky." Excerpt from *The Year of Finding Memory* by Judy Fong Bates (Random House, pp. 26-30).

"The Same Roof." Excerpt from *The Concubine's Children* by Denise Chong (Penguin second edition, 2006: pp 224-227). Copyright © 1994 Denise Chong. With permission of the author.

"Making up Mother." Excerpt from *Belonging* by Isabel Huggan (Vintage Canada) pp 235-237.

"Something Different" by Frances Boyle was previously published in *Oblique Strokes*, Wellington Street Poets (ed. Barbara Myers), Fire Grass Press, 2008.

"A Taste of Lemon" by Rosemary Clewes, *The Dalhousie Review*, Autumn Issue, 2006.

"Lives Lived: Mary (Foley) Doyle" by Marjorie Doyle. This piece first appeared in the *Globe and Mail*.

"Royal Jelly," "Solo," "The Sour Red Cherries" by Marilyn Gear Pilling. Poems previously appeared in *The Bones of the World Begin to Show* (Black Moss Press).

"Manhattan" by Clarissa Green was previously published in *Emerge: The Writer's Studio Anthology*, 2007. Simon Fraser University, Vancouver, BC.

"Moving" by Elizabeth Greene, was previously published in her collection *Moving* (Inanna, 2012).

"Combustion" by Lorri Neilsen Glenn from *Combustion* (Brick Books, 2007)

"Geranium" by Lorri Neilsen Glenn from *Combustion* (Brick Books, 2007). Originally published in *Grain Magazine* (Short Grain Award).

Water to Water by Margaret Zielinski won 1st place in the Dan Sullivan Memorial Poetry Context and was published in Word Weaver, September, 2001.

CONTRIBUTORS

JANICE ACTON

Janice Acton grew up in the 1950s on a small mixed farm in southern Saskatchewan. After graduating from the University of Saskatchewan in 1972, she moved to Toronto. Since 1994 Janice has been living in Halifax, working as a writer and researcher. *The Forward Look* is one of a series of creative non-fiction stories Janice has written for a memoir entitled *Fertile Ground: A 1950s Prairie Memoryscape.*

LEANNE AVERBACH

Leanne Averbach is a poet and experimental filmmaker and has performed her work with musicians across Canada, New York City and Italy. She has written two volumes of poetry, *Fever* (Mansfield Press, 2005) and *Come Closer* (Tightrope Books, 2010) and two films, *Carwash and Teacups & Mink.* Her poetry and films have won awards. For more information see www.leanneaverbach.com.

JANET BARKHOUSE

Janet Barkhouse has published two books. *Riddlefence, CV2, Room, Leaf* and others have published her work. She has studied at the Banff Writing Studio with Jan Zwicky and Barry Dempster, and with Lorri Neilsen Glenn and Kimmy Beach in Sfakia, Crete. Her mother, Joyce Barkhouse, CM, ONS, was both a fine writer and a peach. Janet's most recent book, *Pit Pony: The Picture Book,* is co-authored with her late mother.

FRANCES BOYLE

Frances Boyle's poetry and fiction have appeared in *The Fiddlehead, Room, Moonset, Bywords, Freefall* and *Contemporary Verse 2, The*

New Quarterly, online in *Ottawater 8,* as a LeafPress.ca Monday's poem, and in several anthologies. She was awarded *Arc*'s Diana Brebner Prize, and won first for poetry and third for fiction in *This Magazine*'s Great Canadian Literary Hunt, and second place in *Prairie Fire*'s Banff Centre Bliss Carmen Poetry Award. Happily making her home in Ottawa, Frances draws on strong ties to Regina and Vancouver.

KATE BRAID

Kate Braid has written poetry and non-fiction about subjects from Georgia O'Keeffe, Emily Carr and Glenn Gould, to mine workers and fishers. In addition to co-editing with Sandy Shreve, *In Fine Form,* she has published five books of poetry, most recently *A Well-Mannered Storm: The Glenn Gould Poems* and *Turning Left to the Ladies.* Her memoir of fifteen years as a carpenter, *Journey Woman,* was published in 2012. Her work has won and been short-listed for a number of awards and is widely anthologized.

CAROL BRUNEAU

Happily married and the proud mother of three sons, Carol Bruneau still calls the same Halifax neighbourhood home, though she has travelled and lived in several other cities. She's the author of five books including the acclaimed novels, *Purple for Sky* and *Glass Voices,* and is currently at work on her fourth novel.

SHAUNA BUTTERWICK

Shauna Butterwick, post-WWII baby, born in Pincher Creek, Alberta, has worked as a nurse, peer counsellor, adult educator and academic. She lives in East Vancouver, cares for her ancient cat, her partner, and is a closet poet. Her mother, Jessie Butterwick, born in 1913 in Paisley Scotland, was a short story writer, occasional poet, and homemaker who succumbed to the ravages of Alzheimer's Disease in 1988.

SUE CHENETTE

Sue Chenette is a poet and classical pianist who grew up in northern Wisconsin and has made her home in Toronto since 1972. She is the author of *The Bones of His Being* (Guernica Editions, 2012) and *Slender Human Weight* (Guernica Editions, 2009), as well as three chapbooks: *Solitude in Cloud and Sun, A Transport of Grief,* and *The Time Between Us,* which won the Canadian Poetry Association's Shaunt Basmajian Award in 2001.

DENISE CHONG
Denise Chong's memoir, *The Concubine's Children,* was a Globe and Mail bestseller for 93 weeks. A two-time finalist for the Governor-General's literary award, she is also the author of *The Girl in the Picture: The Story of Kim Phuc,* the *Photograph,* and the *Vietnam War* and *Egg on Mao: A Story of Love, Hope and Defiance,* about the life of a bus mechanic's family.

ROSEMARY CLEWES
Rosemary Clewes lives in Toronto and published her first book of poetry, *Once Houses Could Fly* (Signature Editions) in May 2012. In 2008, she published a book of prose and poetry called *The Arctic Explorer: Kayaking North of 77 Degrees* (Hidden Brook Press). She has travelled the Arctic by kayak, raft and icebreaker.

PAT CLIFFORD
Pat Clifford was an award-winning educator and the author of the poetry collection *Embracing Brings You Back* (Coteau Books). She was raised in Regina and Saskatoon and most recently lived in Calgary, Alberta. Pat died in 2008.

MARY JANE COPPS
Mary Jane Copps is a Halifax-based writer and entrepreneur. Her creative non-fiction has appeared in the anthologies, *Dropped Threads II* and *Nobody's Mother,* as well as several literary journals.

CINDY DEAN-MORRISON
Cindy Dean-Morrison was born and raised on a farm in Saskatchewan and earned both Bachelor of Education and Bachelor of Arts degrees at the University of Regina. She lives in Saskatoon with her husband and two daughters and teaches at Saskatoon Misbah School. Her work has been published in *Grain, Western People, The Observer,* Spring Vol. I, *Our Times* magazine, and has been broadcast on CBC radio. A second-place win in an international "Poetry at Work" contest led to publication in

The Minnesota Review. The majority of her work comes from her rural roots.

MARJORIE DOYLE

A National Magazine Award winner, Marjorie Doyle has published in *Geist, Queen's Quarterly, Fiddlehead, Antigonish Review* and *Descant*. The former *Globe and Mail* columnist and CBC broadcaster has read across Canada and in 2009 was Haig-Brown Writer-in-Residence at Campbell River, BC. Her fourth book, *A Doyle Reader: Essays from Home and Away*, is due for release (Boulder Publications) May, 2013. Now she's working on a book about her mother. Visit Marjorie at www.marjoriedoyle.ca.

JUDY FONG BATES

Judy Fong Bates is the author of the critically acclaimed short-story collection, *China Dog and Other Stories*, and the novel, *Midnight at the Dragon Café*, which was featured by Toronto Public Library as its One Book in 2011. Her family memoir, *The Year of Finding Memory*, was a *2010 Globe 100*.

CYNTHIA FRENCH

Cynthia French's poems have been published in *Riddle Fence, CV2, The New Quarterly*, and the anthology, *The Wild Weathers: A Gathering of Love Poems* (Leaf Press, 2012). She continues to muse on the expectations imposed on women who lived through the Fifties, how they affected her mother and succeeding generations.

MYRNA GARANIS

Myrna Garanis is an Edmonton poet whose work has appeared in *CV2, Room of One's Own*, in a dozen anthologies, and in the collection *Eyeing the Magpie*. She grew up in rural Saskatchewan.

MARILYN GEAR PILLING

Marilyn Gear Pilling lives in Hamilton, Ontario and is the author of six books. Her most recent work of fiction is *The Roseate Spoonbill of Happiness* (2002) and of poetry, *The Bones of the World Begin to Show* (2009). A fifth book of poetry will be out from Cormorant Books in 2013. Her fiction, poetry, and creative nonfiction have been anthologized and have appeared in most of Canada's literary magazines. She has read her work widely, across Canada, and at "Shakespeare & Company" in Paris, France. Her work is upcoming in *The Malahat Review*, *The Dalhousie Review* and *The Antigonish Review*.

CLARISSA GREEN

Clarissa P. Green's poetry, fiction and creative nonfiction explore the interface between time, memory and personal relationships. A therapist, university teacher and graduate of The Writers' Studio at Simon Fraser University, she is a winner of the Vancouver International Writers' Festival contest for fiction. She is completing a creative non-fiction manuscript that explores relationship changes as parents age and die and their children do—or don't—show up.

ELIZABETH GREENE

Elizabeth Greene has published two collections of poetry, *The Iron Shoes* (Hidden Brook, 2007) and *Moving* (Inanna, 2010). She has work forthcoming in several anthologies, including Guernica's *Poet to Poet* Anthology. She lives in Kingston, ON with her son and three cats.

SYLVIA HAMILTON

Sylvia D. Hamilton is Nova Scotian filmmaker and writer whose award-winning films have been screened in Canada and abroad. Her writing appears in a variety of books and journals. Her most recent film is *The Little Black School House*. She teaches part-time in the School of Journalism at the University of King's College in Halifax.

CARLA HARTSFIELD

Carla Hartsfield was born in Waxahachie, Texas, and is a classically-trained pianist, poet, singer-songwriter and visual artist. Her poetry collection, *The Invisible Moon* (Signal Editions/ Vehicule) was short-listed for the LCP Gerald Lampert prize. *Your Last Day on Earth* (Brick Books) was long-listed for the B.C. Relit Awards. Her work has been published in the *Literary Review of Canada*, *Prairie Fire*, *CV2*, *Rampike*, *The Fiddlehead*, *The Antigonish Review*, and *The Malahat Review*. Her chapbook, *The River*, appeared from

Rubicon Press in 2011. Also a recording artist, Carla is working on her second CD with new band, Court the Clouds.

SUSAN HELWIG
Susan L. Helwig grew up on a farm just outside of Neustadt, Ontario. Her two published collections are *Catch the Sweet* (Seraphim Editions, 2001) and *Pink Purse Girl* (Wolsak and Wynn, 2006). A third collection—*And the cat says*—will be published by Quattro Books in spring 2013.

LEKKIE HOPKINS
Lekkie Hopkins is the author of *On Voice and Silence* (2009) and *Among the Chosen: The Life Story of Pat Giles* (2010). She is a Senior Lecturer in Women's Studies at Edith Cowan University in Perth, Australia, and the recipient of national and local awards for her teaching and activism.

ISABEL HUGGAN
Isabel Huggan is a Canadian writer of prize-winning fiction (*The Elizabeth Stories* and *You Never Know*) and memoir (*Belonging: Home Away From Home*). She also publishes essays and poetry. She has been an instructor for the Humber School for Writers since 1998, the same year she settled in the south of France, the site of her writer's retreat (www.isabelhuggan.com).

MAUREEN HYNES
Maureen Hynes' poetry has won the Petra Kenny and Gerald Lampert Awards. Her most recent book is *Marrow, Willow* (Pedlar Press, 2012).

EVE JOSEPH
Eve Joseph's latest collection of poetry is *The Secret Signature of Things* (Brick, 2010). Her first collection was nominated for the Dorothy Livesay Award. She lives in Brentwood Bay, BC.

PENN KEMP
Activist, performer and playwright, Penn Kemp is the League of Canadian Poets' 2012 honourary Life Member and the inaugural

Poet Laureate for the City of London, Ontario. Her book, *Jack Layton: Art in Action* (quattrobooks.ca), launched in May, 2012. She received the Queen Elizabeth Diamond Jubilee Award for contributions to Canadian arts and culture. See www.mytown.ca/pennletters for updates.

ZÖE LANDALE

Zöe Landale is the author of collections of poetry, short fiction, and nonfiction. She lives in Richmond, BC.

MARSHA LEDERMAN

Marsha Lederman is a writer and critic for the *Globe and Mail.*

DEB LOUGHEAD

Toronto writer and poet Deb Loughead credits the resonant storytelling of her mother, Laurie Symsyk, for her enduring enchantment with wordplay. Deb is the award-winning author of more than 25 books for children and young adults, many in translation internationally, and co-editor of *Cleavage: Breakaway Fiction for Real Girls* (Sumach Press 2008). She has written extensively for the Children's Educational market. Visit her website at www.DebLoughead.ca.

JEANETTE LYNES

Jeanette Lynes is the author of six collections of poetry and one novel. Her most recent book of poetry is *Archive of the Undressed* (2012). Her novel, *The Factory Voice* (2009) was long-listed for the Scotiabank Giller Prize. She is Coordinator of the MFA in Writing at the University of Saskatchewan.

ALICE MAJOR

Alice Major has published nine highly-praised poetry collections for which she has won prizes such as the Pat Lowther and Stephan G. Stephansson Awards. Her latest book is a collection of essays, *Intersecting Sets: A Poet Looks at Science,* for which she has won the Wilfrid Eggleston Award, and also a National Magazine Award. She served as the first poet laureate for her home city of Edmonton.

ALLISON MARION
A passionate reader growing up, Allison began to put feelings onto paper in 2008 as part therapy, part curiosity. In 2011, she retired from a successful 40-year banking career to spend more time with her family and friends, and to continue pursuing her interests of writing and interior design.

DAPHNE MARLATT
Daphne Marlatt has published more than twenty books of poetry, fiction, oral history, and theory. She was the co-founder of groundbreaking journals, *Tessera* and *periodics*, and an editor on several other journals. Her narrative poem, *The Given*, received the 2009 Dorothy Livesay Poetry Award. The 2006 Pangaea Arts production of her contemporary Canadian Noh play, *The Gull*, was awarded the international Uchimura Naoya Theatre Prize. In 2011, *Shadow Catch*, a Noh-based chamber opera with new music, for which she wrote the libretto, was produced by Pro Musica in Vancouver. She is currently working on *Liquidities: Vancouver Poems Then and Now*, forthcoming from Talonbooks in 2013. Daphne was awarded the Order of Canada in 2006 for her contributions to Canadian literature.

RHONA McADAM
Rhona McAdam has lived in BC, Edmonton and London, England, and spent a year studying food in Italy. Her poetry collections include two food poetry chapbooks, *Sunday Dinners* (JackPine, 2010) and *The Earth's Kitchen* (Leaf, 2011). Oolichan Books published her fifth full-length collection, *Cartography*, in 2006. Her first book of nonfiction, *Digging the City: An Urban Agriculture Manifesto*, was published in 2012 by Rocky Mountain Books.

LYNDA MONAHAN
Lynda is the author of two collections of poetry, *A Slow Dance in the Flames* and *What My Body Knows*, both published by Coteau Books. Lynda teaches creative writing at SIAST Woodland Campus in Prince Albert, SK and facilitates a variety of writing workshops.

JANE MUNRO
A native of BC, Jane Munro's fifth poetry collection is *Active Pass* (2010). It explores connections among the visual arts, yogic

discipline, and self-regeneration. Munro is a member of Yoko's Dogs, a poetry collective working in the tradition of renku; Pedlar Press recently released *Whisk*, their first collection. htttp://janemunro.com

SARAH MURPHY

Interpreter; translator; community activist; award-winning performance, visual and spoken word artist, Sarah Murphy is the widely anthologized author of eight books of nonfiction, fiction and cross-over genres that include drawing and photo-montage as well as dramatic monologues and prose poems. A long term resident of Canada, Mexico and the United States, in 2007 she received an Arts Council England International Artists Fellowship to produce her sound art CD *when bill danced the war,* and in 2009 published her latest book, an innovative memoir of a Brooklyn childhood in lyric prose, *Last Taxi to Nutmeg Mews*. She makes her home in Bocabec, New Brunswick.

LORRI NEILSEN GLENN

Lorri Neilsen Glenn is the author and editor of thirteen collections of nonfiction and poetry, the most recent being a bricolage of poetry and memoir, *Threading Light: Explorations in Loss and Poetry* (Hagios Press, 2011) and *Lost Gospels* (Brick, 2010). Her poetry and creative nonfiction have appeared in and won a number of awards in publications including *The Malahat Review, Grain, Prairie Fire, CV2,* and *Event*. She is the former Poet Laureate of Halifax, Nova Scotia. She teaches poetry and creative nonfiction in Canada and abroad.

SHEILA NORGATE

Sheila Norgate was born in downtown Toronto in 1950 at the height of the post-war frenzy to corral women back into the home. It was a time when girls were turned on the lathe of home economics and spun into teachers, nurses, secretaries and housewives. In the midst of an accidental and bland career in banking, Norgate suffered a major health crisis and began to dabble in art. She now paints full-time from her home on Gabriola Island, BC. Norgate's other passion is vintage etiquette aimed at women. She has scripted several one-woman shows in a desperate attempt to redeem those girls who have let themselves go. She is the author of *Storm Clouds*

Over Party Shoes, Etiquette Problems for the Ill-Bred Woman, Press Gang, 1997.

JOANNE PAGE

Joanne Page is a writer and visual artist who lives in Kingston. She grew up in the centre of Toronto. Her collections of poetry are *The River & The Lake* (Quarry Press), *Persuasion for a Mathematician* and *Watermarks* (Pedlar Press). *Watermarks* was short-listed for the 2008 Trillium Award and a section was short-listed for the CBC literary awards.

E. ALEX PIERCE

E. Alex Pierce lives in Nova Scotia. Her poems have won or been short-listed for several Canadian and international awards. Her poetry collection *Vox Humana* was published by Brick Books in 2011 and is now in its second printing.

RUTH ROACH PIERSON

Professor emeritus of the University of Toronto/ Ontario Institute for Studies in Education, Ruth Roach Pierson taught women's history, feminist studies, and post-colonial studies at OISE/UT from 1980 to 2001, and European history and women's history at Memorial University of Newfoundland from 1970 to 1980. She has published three poetry collections: *Where No Window Was* (BuschekBooks, 2002) and *Aide-Mémoire* (BuschekBooks, 2007), which was a finalist for the 2008 Governor General's Literary Award for Poetry, and *Contrary* (Tightrope Books, 2011). She is editing an anthology of movie poems entitled *I Found it at the Movies* to be published by Guernica Editions.

MARILYNN RUDI

Marilynn Rudi lives and works in Dartmouth, Nova Scotia. By day, she's a librarian/archivist at the Bedford Institute of Oceanography. By night, she's a writer. Marilynn has published poems in *The New Quarterly, The Antigonish Review* and *The Nashwaak Review*. She was born sometime in the 1950s.

DEBORAH SCHNITZER

Deborah's work includes the anthology *Madwoman in the Academy*, the novel, *an unexpected break in the weather*, and the experimental short film, *Canoe*. Current pieces taking shape involve a collaborative novel composed by 15 writers, *At The Edge*, a project designed with Marjorie Anderson, and *set to paper*, a film with director Shelagh Carter, developed in response to Gertrude Stein's invitation to dance.

DIANE SCHOEMPERLEN

Diane Schoemperlen is the author of three novels, one book of non-fiction, and several collections of short stories including *Forms of Devotion: Stories and Pictures*, which won the Governor-General's Award for English Fiction in 1998. Her most recent book is *At A Loss For Words: A Post-Romantic Novel*. In 2008 she received the Marian Engel Award. Originally from Thunder Bay, Ontario, she now lives in Kingston, where she was Writer-in-Residence at Queen's University in 2012.

MARJORIE SIMMINS

Marjorie Simmins is an award-winning writer based in Halifax, Nova Scotia. She has worked as a freelance journalist and writing instructor for over twenty years, writing often about family, marine life, animals and coastal living. Her articles and essays have appeared in magazines and newspapers across Canada and the U.S. and in several anthologies.

BETSY STRUTHERS

Betsy Struthers has published nine books of poetry—most recently *All That Desire: New and Selected Poems* (Black Moss Press, 2012)—three novels, and a book of short fiction. She also co-edited and contributed to a book of essays about teaching poetry. She is a past president of the League of Canadian Poets. Winner of the 2010 GritLit Poetry Award, the 2004 Lowther Award for the best book of poetry by a Canadian woman, and silver medalist for the 1994 Milton Acorn Memorial People's Poetry Award, her poems and fiction have been published in many literary journals and anthologies. Struthers lives in Peterborough, Ontario, where she works as a freelance editor.

SHARON THESEN

Sharon Thesen is a BC-based poet and editor. Her books of poetry include *Oyama Pink Shale, The Good Bacteria*, and *News &*

Smoke: Selected Poems; and she is the editor, among other books, of *The New Long Poem Anthology*. She taught for many years at Capilano College in North Vancouver and is now a professor in the Department of Creative Studies at UBC's Okanagan campus.

PAM THOMAS
Pam Thomas was born in America and moved to England in 1947. She worked in publishing until her retirement. She has contributed many articles in a variety of UK publications. She lives in Oxford with her husband, and has three children and four grandchildren.

DAVI WALDERS
Davi Walders' work has been nominated for Pushcart Prizes, read by Garrison Keillor, and widely anthologized. She is the author of *Women Against Tyranny: Poems of Resistance during the Holocaust* (Clemson University Digital Press, 2011). She lives in Maryland.

CYNTHIA WOODMAN KERKHAM
Cynthia Woodman Kerkham was raised in Toronto, Hong Kong and Vancouver by a beautifully-dressed mother and has worked as an au pair in France, a potter, a journalist and a teacher. Her poems have won awards. *Good Holding Ground*, her debut collection of poems, was published in spring 2011 by Palimpsest Press.

PATRICIA YOUNG
Patricia Young has published nine collections of poetry, most recently, *Here Come the Moonbathers* (Biblioasis, 2008) and one collection of short fiction, *Airstream*, which won the Rooke-Metcalf Award and was included on the Globe and Mail's list of best books of the year (2006). In 2008 she won prizes in the *Prairie Fire, Grain* and *Room of One's Own* literary contests. She also won *Arc*'s Poem of the Year Contest. She lives in Victoria, BC. *[A section in this anthology is titled "The Mad and Beautiful Mothers," after the award-winning book of poetry by Young published in 1989 (Ragweed Press)].*

LIZ ZETLIN
Liz Zetlin is the author of five poetry collections. Her most recent are *The Punctuation Field* (Black Moss) and *The Thing With Feathers*

(Buschek Books). Her poetry has won national awards (e.g. Stephen Leacock, Shaunt Basmajian) and she has produced many poetry videos as well as an award-winning feature documentary: *Words Aloud*. She was Owen Sound's inaugural poet laureate (2007-2008) and co-founder/artistic director of the Words Aloud Spoken Word Festival (www.wordsaloud.ca).

MARGARET ZIELINSKI

Born in Scotland, Margaret Malloch Zielinski lives now in Ottawa. Her work has appeared in several anthologies as well as in *The Antigonish Review, Bywords, Contemporary Verse 2, The Dalhousie Review, Geist, Quills,* and *Room.* Together with five other Fieldstone Poets, she recently published a collection of travel poetry, *Whistle for Jellyfish* (Bookland Press, Toronto).